A Country For Old Men

And Other Stories

E.R. Zietlow

Lame Johnny Press

Previous publications of stories in this volume include the following: "Waiting" in **Canadian Short Fiction Anthology;** "Winter Wheat" in **The Literature of South Dakota;** "Winter Wheat" and "The Burial of the Bride" in **South Dakota Review;** "Silver: in the **Journal of Canadian Fiction;** "The Old Woman Who Read to Her House Plants" and "Etta Jimson" in **Revue II.**

Library of Congress number: 76-582-38

ISBN 0-917624-05-X, hardcover, $4.95
ISBN 0-917624-02-5, paperback, $2.95

Lame Johnny Press
Box 66 Hermosa SD 57744

A Country For Old Men

There is no excellent beauty that hath not some strangeness in the proportion.

—Sir Francis Bacon

And Other Stories

This book is for the family:

Mother, Alvin and Janet, Alfred,

Lloyd and Ceci.

Silver

Out of a dozen eggs, seven chicks had hatched, and one of them was spraddle-legged. Silver cracked its head on the coop and gave it a throw. She had kept the hen locked in until all the good eggs hatched. Now she opened the gate. The hen clucked her brood across ground that was largely bare; a yard amid tired barns and sheds set in raw country. The hen pecked; the chicks pecked.

Silver, on her knees, drew out the bad eggs gingerly. White-haired since adolescence, she looked twenty years beyond her bony forty-three. A trace of Indian blood sharpened her features just percept-ibly. Her dress, once mauve, was now the bleached gray of the earth. Like her, it had faded early. "Well, ain't going to be many fryers this year. I suppose the old man'll bawl me out. My fault that the eggs didn't hatch." Not wholly aware of it, she had begun talking to a large tomcat stretched on the ground a few yards away. He watched her half upside down. "I guess I'd better bury these. You get them, you'll be sucking eggs in the hen house. Old man catches you doing that, he'll take the shotgun to you." She had trouble balancing the eggs in her arthritic fingers.

With a spade from the tool shed, she dug a hole at the end of her garden. As an afterthought, she put the dead chick in too. "You eat him, and then you'll be chasing the others," she told the cat. It rolled playfully on its back. "Yeah! You act pretty cozy! Touch them chicks, and that old hen'll pull your tail out by the roots."

Off some yards, the hen had made a discovery. She clucked in sharpened tempo, and the chicks around her yeeped and pecked. They were golden in the bright sun.

Silver watched for a minute and then went into the house. In the front room, her last-born, three, unexpected, unwanted, a dwarf and an idiot, sprawled in his play pen. When he looked at her, his head did not stay still. If he tried to crawl or pull himself up, his legs twisted uselessly. But his hands were fairly strong. He gurgled and bubbled mucus in his nostrils.

Silver bent over him and checked his diaper. It was soiled. "Well, I guess I'm going to have to give you a bath," she said. "Time for a bath anyway. You are a mess, aren't you?"

She put a teakettle and a pot of water on the stove — then set a waterpail on too. From outside, she got a washtub and put it in the middle of the floor. There was time for her to carry two pails of cold water from the well; time yet to wait and test the heating water with a finger. "Give you a good soaking once," she told the child. Usually he got bathed with a pan and a washcloth.

All the pails and kettles filled the tub substantially. The child made happy gurgles. Silver began scrubbing with her soap and rag. "That's right. Hang onto the side. I'll wash your head too, long's I got all this water." Kneeling was a painful position for her, but she was not in the habit of sparing herself.

Sudden commotion outside; angry squawking.

"Goddamned cat!" She shot up like a jack from a box despite her stiffness. Bolting for the door, she flung back the washcloth and a sharp command. "You sit tight!"

Outside, mother hen faced off the cat. Hunched and hackled like a fighting cock, she guarded the huddling chicks. Her adversary, head cocked reflectively, seemed undismayed. The tip of his tail flicked this way and that.

Silver snatched up a stone. "Damn you!" she raged, "leave them chicks alone! I stew over that hen to get six eggs hatched, and then you try to gobble them up. The old man'll raise hell. Go chase the mice for once!" She threw. The cat fled. But at a fence, he stopped, long and panther-like, turning back to watch.

Silver paused. "Minute I'm gone, you'll be up to your tricks again, won't you? If I could catch you now, I'd put you on a chain." To the hen, she said: "Have to lock you up till the chicks get bigger. Damn that cat." Having intended to return immediately, she was torn and couldn't think any better than she could when Raul swore and shouted at her. Because she was there, outside, she grabbed a handful of wheat from her feed bucket and scattered it before and inside the coop. Controlling her urgency, she drove the hen that way. But the hen was riled up and didn't see the grain. Silver cursed and drove her back again. This time she clucked and pecked and followed the trail of wheat into the coop, chicks scampering around her. Silver locked the little gate.

Panic hit her when she turned to the house. Legs flying awkwardly, she shot up the steps. It seemed now that a good deal of time had passed.

Enough at least. It was a big tub and a lot of water. He had got his legs behind him somehow, and his face under. Silver plucked him out and jacknifed him. She felt for his heart; felt for his pulse. There was no life remaining.

Silver ran out of the house screaming: "Raul! Raul!" But he was riding somewhere in the south pastures. Sunny and Rusty, her older children, were also gone, and with them, Bootie, Sunny's child. She scurried back and forth, wanting Raul to be there, wanting the definitive reality of his rage. Doing nothing was unbearable — yet there was nothing to do.

She resolved to drive to the city herself, but quickly realized the trip was useless for the child's sake. Still, some kind of desperate action seemed morally required. She charged into the house; charged out again. Dinner! They would want dinner! Back in again. Stoke the fire. Peel potatoes. But no, they would have to leave right away. She threw the potatoes out. Wasting potatoes! She gathered them up again and washed them off and covered them with water.

She stood still. The world had been normal and natural — then all at once it had turned a different face. It had caught her out. She felt there must be a reason, and she tried to get hold of it. The chicks had **had** to be looked after. Taking care of the place was the single inviolable commandment, which welded the family together, and they all knew it. But the idiot child had never shared that. He was a different side of things. In the midst of tumult, she glimpsed a quiet spot within her and quickly shut it away.

When Raul came home, Silver ran to him and tried to explain. It had been an accident. Yet her words did not seem to describe an accident. One did not accidentally leave such a child in a washtub.

"Jesus Christ!" Raul shouted.

The more Silver talked, the less clear things were, and the more agitated she became — and the faster she talked. There was pain in her body; pain in her joints.

In the house, Raul looked at the dead boy and turned frightened eyes on Silver. He stormed up and down, shouting: "Jesus Christ, woman! Jesus Christ!"

He carried the boy out to the car. Silver left a note for Sunny and Rusty. Then they drove toward the city, both of them hunched forward, Raul on top of the wheel and going fast. "Hell, I don't know what they're going to say about this," he burst out. "I don't know if they're going to believe you or not. They might have you in court. Goddamnit, woman, you got to look after a kid like that a little bit!"

Silver found both fear and comfort in the idea of a trial. If they put her in jail, she would be paying, and that would take care of everything.

They took the child to the hospital, even though it was dead. After Silver answered questions and their doctor examined the body and made a report to the coroner, they knew there would be no inquest or trial. Raul got ready to leave. But Silver told him her arthritis was bothering. Trembling at her audacity, yet making her stand, she asked to stay in the hospital a few days. The doctor talked to her alone; then told Raul he thought it best that she stay.

Next day, when the doctor visited, she was more free with him. Sitting on the edge of the bed, she told him: "It was an acident. I know that. But I don't think **he** believes that. I wouldn't be surprised if **he** thinks I let the poor little tyke drown. I've got a little Indian blood in me, you know. Just a little. But it bothers **him.** Sunny was blonde — the girl, you know, the oldest. And then Rusty was a redhead, and naturally **he** got to thinking that's the way our kids should be — should take after **him.** Well, this little one came along and he was dark — not **real** dark, but dark. I was dark too, before my hair went white. My dad was dark, and he didn't have no Indian in him. Well, then, the little tyke wasn't right either. Couldn't control himself. So I suppose **he** thought that was because of me — because of the Indian in me or something. And I suppose **he** thinks that's what I was trying to do — drown the kid because I'm ashamed of it. Why should I be ashamed? It's nothing I did, is it? It's just **there.** It could happen to anyone. But **he's** funny. **He's** funny." She talked fast and plucked at the blanket. After a moment she shook her head vigorously: "He's funny!"

The doctor didn't say anything.

Soon she began again. "I don't know. I don't know. It seems

to me there's been something funny with this marriage from the beginning. I don't see that he's ever acted like a man should. The money, that's all his. He keeps all that. Well, that's all right. I don't care. If it means that much to him, let him have it. But he keeps to himself. He's funny. Don't tell me what he's up to most of the time. You'd think he was suspicious of me. Suspicious of everybody. I don't know what he wants.

"It's something to live with, I'll tell the world. I've got this arthritis, but I'm expected to take care of the house, take care of the chickens, take care of the garden. Sometimes I'm expected to help with the haying or the cows too. It gets to be just about too much for me. And Rusty's getting big. But he don't let him work. Not like he should; not sharing. Then there's Bootie, too, Sunny's little girl. He blows up and cusses around her just the way he does around the rest of us.

"And he's so dead set against Indians. His way of trying to get under my skin, I think. Well, I don't care. It don't bother me. But why did he marry me if he was going to be like that, huh? What's the matter with him? If he's so dead set against Indian blood, why does he marry Indian blood? Does that make sense to you? It don't to me. There's very little about **him** that does make sense to me."

The doctor nodded. He suggested perhaps she should talk to Dr. Haight. Later that afternoon, Dr. Haight was at the hospital and saw her briefly. Silver pretty much repeated what she had said before.

Dr. Haight asked her how she felt about Indians.

She assured him that she would have nothing to do with them. "I'm not Indian! You have to go back to my grandmother before you get much Indian."

Did she think the child looked Indian?

"Certainly not! Well . . . I suppose you could say it did — if you were thinking of its complexion. No. No, it didn't look Indian at all!"

How had Raul felt toward the child?

"I don't think he had any feelings. Well . . . he didn't like it we had him, but he was tolerant. He was tolerant."

Dr. Haight explained about projection. Maybe, he said, Raul had wished — unconsciously — at one time that the child were not with them. Maybe he projected that wish onto Silver. That was just a maybe, of course.

Dr. Haight invited her to make an appointment at his office if she wanted to talk further — right now he had a patient to see down the hall.

After he left, Silver puzzled over what had been said. She felt uneasy, unsure that she had answered the questions right. Especially regarding how she felt about Indians. The business about Raul accusing her . . . well, **believing** about her what was true of him pleased her at first. But then she got the uncanny feeling that Dr. Haight hadn't been trying to comfort her. He had switched it around somehow and was really talking about her. She couldn't figure it out — didn't want to — but she felt at the bayonet point of accusation. **Everything had been her fault all along the way —** blinding! And the quiet spot opened inside her.

Twenty-five years ago, out of loneliness and a naive faith that everything would be all right if she were married, she had let Raul use her. When her period had not come "on time," she had panicked him into marriage. Only some months later had she really become pregnant.

But she had been young and innocent too!

She recalled lying beside Raul in their bed during the early years of the marriage, feeling some fear of him because of the way he talked to her and treated her. Later, she had understood him more. She had understood his weaknesses, his jealousies, his failings. He irritated her, and she came to know the right moment to turn away in pretended ignorance of his desire for her. Then he was grumpy and found fault with her, and so it went.

The children were born by then, and the children grew. She turned to them; especially Rusty. She thought about him grown up. He could live on a neighboring place. Maybe he would meet some shy girl hoeing in a garden as Raul had. Only Rusty would act like a man should toward his shy, lonesome girl. They would marry and have children and bring the children to see her.

In a way Silver never understood, Raul did not get along with Rusty. The boy drew his anger. And if Rusty's work around the place was at issue, Silver found it very difficult to give Raul's complaint a hearing. She did not want Rusty to be wrong. She asked questions, not affronting Raul, not defending Rusty, but undercutting Raul's arguments — and usually his attitude was overly sharp. He made too much of things. Rusty picketed a saddle horse that was not broke to picket. It got a ropeburn in the pastern. Raul was mad. Silver shrugged it off, being completely practical. Is there no other horse for him to ride? That wasn't the point, said Raul. Oh? What was the point? Boys will be boys. He won't likely do it again. He has to learn. She knew it galled him when she shrugged things off.

With Sunny it was different. She went to high school, and when she got out, came back to the place and did more outside work than house work. Just how close to her dad she was, Silver couldn't judge. Sunny did not usually ride with him, but he criticized her less than Rusty. He let her have more things. She got to buy a saddle, while Rusty had to take an old one. She also got the pick of the horses — other than Raul's mare.

Sometimes Silver nagged her daughter, saying she ought to help out in the house more. Sometimes, when they were both gone, she wondered if Raul and Sunny were riding together. What would he be telling her?

When Sunny got pregnant, Silver was indignant and concerned about what people would think. It was an ironic playback of an earlier scene. Sunny had always been Raul's girl; now he wondered aloud what "that girl of yours" had been up to.

He forced a marriage and divorce as fast as they could follow each other, and a bit of time passed, and Silver felt quite differently about the matter. Sunny would soon necessarily be around the house more. She would not be around Raul. Silver began to have talks with her about the baby. She encouraged Sunny to demand things of Raul — a new stove, new furnishings for her bedroom. Aligning herself with Sunny, with the expected baby, Silver counted as she never had before. Silver befriended her daughter; it was a new and different relationship. She found that the baby was something to look forward to, something to plan for. Her life became happier.

But Raul shared in this mellowing, and he and Silver were brought back together. Unprepared for such an eventuality, Silver found herself pregnant. That dampened the Indian summer of their love; the defective baby ended it for good. Silver moved upstairs into a different bedroom.

But before that happened, Sunny had a beautiful baby and named her Sarah, for princess — Silver called her Bootie. Reconciled to her own pregnancy, Silver felt close to her daughter; there was a mysterious parallel. When the child turned out to be defective, that was erased. She felt isolated. And by then, Sunny had begun to ride again and work outdoors. Silver took care of Bootie. Sunny let her.

If a meal was late and Raul complained, Silver said: "I was taking care of Bootie. She can't look after herself, you know. I would think that you could a little bit though." She talked about Bootie at the table, and provoked Raul with suggestions about building onto the house.

"She ain't grown up yet," he growled.

"Well, I'm going to see that she's not deprived!"

"Deprived? Who the hell around here was ever deprived?"

"I could name a few!" snapped Silver.

"Bull!"

Once she got him mad enough that he made a remark about the idiot child, calling him "your Indian." In other fights throughout the years, he had let her know that he was less than proud of her Indian blood. She knew that the community at large felt the same way — she was tainted. The taint brought a bitterness, and the bitterness became the taint.

Lying in the hospital bed thinking it over, she felt variously guilty, yet driven to the guilt. Unfair! She wrung a corner of the blanket and wept with rage.

When her doctor came next day, she told him not to send Dr. Haight again. She couldn't afford two of them. Her husband would already be mad because of the bill she had run up. They weren't that well off. In saying "they," she reached back toward her family, to whom she felt closer than she felt to the doctors. She said she had heard bee stings were good for arthritis. Maybe it would be a smart thing to get a hive and keep it on the place.

"I don't think the stings would be any help," said the doctor. "I'll give you a prescription."

Upon leaving the hospital, Silver filled the prescription once. She used aspirin then, but told Raul: "I've seen bee hives along the road; I want to get a hive. I think the stings would cure my arthritis."

"I don't want no damn bees on the place stinging the hell out of me," Raul told her.

"You just like it that I suffer, that's all."

"Hell!" he muttered. "Damned bees would be stinging the horses and stinging us in the hay fields."

"I've never heard of a bee stinging a horse. I'm the only one they'd sting, and that'd be because I'd want it—to cure my arthritis. I'm going to write that fellow and see if I can have a hive."

Some days later, she did write, and the bee keeper, a genial fellow, delivered a hive. He told her they were gentle bees, but added wryly that he didn't think she'd have too much trouble if she **wanted** to get stung.

When the man left, she stood by the hive, apprenhensive but resolute. Nothing happened, and finally she said aloud. "They don't even sting me. **He** must be some kind of sissy, thinking they'd sting him!"

She got a box and sat near the entrance, watching the bees crawl in and out. She put down her hand. One crawled on. When it got over a knuckle, she touched it, and it stung her. The hair-like needle penetrated with a point of fire; then the bee strained until it tore itself loose. Watching very closely, Silver could see the pulsing of the little poison sac. She let it inject all its fluid. With this burning in her knuckle, the arthritic pain seemed diminished. She put out her hand again and got several more bees to sting her. The pain was quite bearable, and that discovery pleased her. Already she felt a special relationship with the perfect little creatures. Strong medicine! With defiant pleasure, she thought of the word in the Indian sense: medicine as magic, power.

When Raul came in, he asked: "What the hell? Did you go and get some bees?"

"Yes!" she snapped. "And they help my arthritis too."

Raul ventured out to look at them with her. She stood unbothered by the hive, but a bee swooped in and stung him behind the ear. He shouted curses. "I was afraid they'd be stinging me."

"Phooey! It's nothing. Like a mosquito bite."

From then on, she spent a good deal of time at the hive. If Raul wanted to talk to her, he did so from a distance. Then she would speak softly, and he would ask what she had said, and she would tell him to come up where he could hear or clean out his ears. Or, while he stood back, complaining about his troubles, whatever they might be, she would smile and let the insects crawl over her hands. He would avert his eyes, with a whining of frustration in his voice. The hive became her refuge. Attacked by arthritis, the family, her sundry anxieties, she fled to the bees and invited their stings.

Bootie was four now, and Silver felt the child growing independent. She began riding in the saddle with Sunny or Rusty, and Silver was left alone. She tried to be good to her grandchild, but Bootie was not always appreciative. When the female cat had kittens, Raul said no; no more cats. They were Bootie's joy, and Silver made a stand. "That poor tyke's got nothing else to play with. I don't see why she can't have a few kittens."

Raul gave in. But Silver felt guilty in her victory and unsure the little girl really cared very much. "Come here, Bootie!" she ventured quite often, and sometimes the little girl cried: "No!" and ran away.

One day Raul brought in a big bull calf that should have been castrated in the spring but somehow was missed. Sunny and Rusty were his help. Silver went to the corral to watch. Bootie, who had been playing with the kittens nearby, joined her. The mother cat came and lay down, rolling this way and that under the fence.

Rusty wanted to rope the calf, but missed, and it nearly jumped the gate. Raul got worked up. "Give me that rope!" he shouted.

The calf went though his loop, and that made him angrier.

Sunny then got a loop around the animal's neck and a half hitch around the snubbing post. Raul got his rope on the heels, and they dragged the calf down. Raul was puffing and sweating and scolding at Rusty. "Where's my knife? Where's that disinfectant? Rusty hadn't had them and didn't know, and amid the cursing and the foolish uproar, Silver at the fence felt violent. She saw where the knife was, but she let Raul find it. Bootie had squatted to pet the mother cat.

Raul set the can of disinfectant out away from the calf and knelt with his pliers and knife. When he flung the first testicle away, the mother cat bounded over to see what had fallen. She gripped it in her teeth and marched triumphantly across the corral. Behind her, leaping and stumbling, went a procession of fur balls. The surface was rough; tramped down hay, dirt, dung, which had been torn by struggling hooves. The kittens bounded and sprawled.

Silver had a premonition of what would happen, but caught ever so briefly on the fulcrum of decision, she said nothing. She waited.

Flinging out the other testicle, wiping his forehead with bloody hands, Raul turned back to get the little tin can of disinfectant. One kitten, seeing a movement, sprang to attack the hand playfully, shunted sideways into the can spilling half its contents. Raul's hand, continuing its motion as if it had had no other objective, swept up the kitten and spun it into the barn twenty feet away. Its tiny legs clawed air, but after the padded thud it dropped like a rag.

Raul stood frozen for a moment. Then he looked at Silver. She tensed but met his eyes until he turned away.

Bootie had already scrambled through the fence and run to the barn. She crouched sobbing over the dead kitten.

Sunny turned hurt, exasperated eyes from Raul to Silver. "Why didn't you keep them out of the corral when he's working? Why didn't you say something? Didn't you see where they were going?"

Buffeted by conscience now, Silver cried: "How did I know they were going to get in **his** way? Does he have to kill everything that interrupts him?"

Raul splashed what little disinfectant remained on the calf. Then he let it loose.

"Could have been worse!" Rusty piped. "Look what happened to the calf!" But he was the only one who tried to laugh.

Raul walked half way to Bootie. "Guess I was a little het up." She only renewed her sobbing. "Plenty more kittens, huh?" He went over to her and fished in his pocket. "Here. Maybe this'll help. You can get a candy bar." She took the coin he offered and threw it as hard as she could.

Silver walked back toward the house. But she passed it and went on to the bee hive. There, she sat watching the bees crawl in and out. She let a few sting her hands.

Then all at once, with a sobbed cry of: "Grandma!" Bootie was there, clutching the dead kitten. She flung herself across her grandmother's lap. Instantly half a dozen bees swooped in and left their stingers on her face and arms. Silver dragged her away and dug out the stingers. But the little girl shrieked in tortured abandon.

Later, in the house, Bootie's eyes swelled shut. Silver ministered to her with cold washclothes under Sunny's reproachful glances.

Timidly, Raul suggested: "You better get rid of them bees now, before they really hurt someone."

"I'll never get rid of them!" she spat back, voice aquiver. "They're all that keeps me from being a complete cripple." She hugged Bootie and dabbed at her face. "They're all that I have.

But she did not want to go back to the hive. She wanted rather to go back to that moment on the fulcrum of decision and cry a warning and save the kitten. She wanted to explain to Sunny that it hadn't been at all the way it had looked.

When Raul was gone and only Sunny was there, Silver ventured: "I sure wouldn't have let them cats get near that corral if I'd known what that man was going to do. You know, he scares me sometimes. Why, kill that poor little tyke's kitten!"

"I'm sure she'll forget about it by tomorrow," Sunny told her wearily.

"But it's not right!"

Sunny gave her such a piercing look that she fell silent and raised one arthritic hand to pinch the sagging dress at her bosom, turning half away, feeling the quiet spot open within, spread outward to the margins of her being.

Waiting

Morna Fehler was in the bedroom dusting a bureau. Her hand struck a ceramic image of a kitten entangled in yarn, given her by her mother years ago. It fell to the rug but didn't break. Yet, with the surprise, she was suddenly weeping — making scarcely any sound; only a jagged, panting breath occasionally punctuated by faint cries, like a very tight door being opened a little at a time. Ross was away. Donnie was on the floor in the front room, where the TV played a variety show Morna liked.

She stooped to get the kitten and put it back, fingering it like a child, taking time to pull herself together. She didn't want Donnie to see her crying. In this vulnerable moment, she experienced above all a need to feel his tender spirit protected — for an alarm had sounded deep inside with the discovery that she was so easily shattered.

Since Donnie's birth, Morna's inner life had centered around the nursery. The child necessarily occupied considerable time. But this time had become more than a proper and rewarding duty: she used it as an essential ballast in her life. The week-by-week progress, the first step, the first word, had to bear meaning for her beyond the intrinsic importance for the child. However, she avoided the self-indulgence of spoiling him, was careful in her attentions, distracted him from things he ought not to have, and instructed him patiently in his eating and playing. Yet, in odd, inexplicable moments, she spanked him rather severely for trivial or accidental misdoing: tearing a magazine, spilling water. Such lapses frightened her, and she was ashamed and silent when Ross came home — although he never criticized her, regardless of what she did with Donnie. Usually when he came in, he talked about people he had met in town, or about land deals, complaining not exactly to her, but just in her presence, seeming unaware of her feeling one way or another. They scarcely communicated on a personal level. Morna never spoke of her emotions.

When her eyes were dry, Morna went into the front room smiling. Donnie flapped his hands, pointing at the TV. "Horsie! Horsie!"

"Horsie?" asked Morna. There was no longer a horse on the screen.

Donnie grinned.

"You charmer!" she told him.

He gurgled indefinite sounds and thumped the floor.

"You singing? You singing?" She sat by him — then lay on her back and boosted him over her at arms' length. "Oh, you're getting big! My, what a big boy! So big!" She rocked him from side to side. "So big!" He puffed and drooled. She hugged him to her. "Momma's big boy! That's what you are." She sat up with him, and held him for a pair of minutes, rubbing his back while she watched the television. Then she put him in his play pen and went into the kitchen.

Life was neither tears nor aftermath now, and she felt disoriented: at a beginning that began nothing. Early in her marriage she had refused to accept her bad moments as meaningful. But they had encroached more and more. And then one day, one warm, unusual day the previous February, in a concrete act of infidelity, she lost the person her mother and her teachers and the minister in town had taught her she was, and she could not again securely believe in her innocence or stability. The sublime control she had managed in her teens was gone, and she waited with a sense of demoniac presence for some more apocalyptic event. Now the tearful outburst had been like a flashing red light. She could perceive no possibility for a change in the marriage, but she felt change in herself, and fear signaled flight, and guilt commanded a patient endurance. The result was apathy. She saw her life, past, present and future, better than she had ever seen it, yet she found herself a spectator.

Morna's father had left when she was fourteen, and she had not heard from him again. He had worked for a house builder in town. The neighborhood joke had it that he was a finisher who kept getting plastered. Frequently he missed supper and came home drunk, sometimes to shout and quarrel with his wife. Or with his children. He was a man of modest stature with a rough-handsome face, blondish hair, hazel eyes — he was Scotch, Harry McKechnie.

The mother was dark complected, fairly tall, and good-looking — Irish in the background, but a Baptist. She spent considerable time in church activities. They were Satan and a righteous angel, balancing each other across a gulf of chaos. Morna, with a child's faith in appearances, had to see her mother as right and her father as wrong, although it was her father to whom she was drawn most naturally. She feared him and felt responsible for him — and often enjoyed him. He took her sometimes to a rodeo, horse show or circus. Her mother took her to church and very rarely anywhere else. But if she made a promise, she kept it; Morna's father gave his word easily and kept it with difficulty. Numerous evenings she sat in a new dress waiting for him to come home and take her and her little brother to a children's movie, a school fair, a fireworks display. Her mother did not make an alternative arrangement so that they could go; she used the occasion to lecture them on their father's unreliability and her own hardships.

When he was sober, Morna's father brought her presents of candy, dolls and books. He made sure she had good clothes. He took her to the dentist while her adult teeth were growing in, and her mouth as a consequence was beautifully straight. He looked after her appearance and called her his angel; her mother said it was more important that she be straight inside, and guided her with a cold hand.

But her teeth were a visible achievement, and her father took every opportunity to show her off. "Let 'em see your teeth, honey!" he boomed, whenever anyone visited the house. "Let 'em see your teeth! I did that. I saw to it that she got to the dentist. Not many fathers no better off than me do that for their kids. Crack a joke in a gang of kids and see what a hell of a looking bunch of mouths you get." Sometimes he caught hold of her and pushed her lips back efficiently, beaming with pride. Afterwards she ran to the bathroom to wash her mouth. And there was a period during which she hid when anyone visited.

When he was drunk, her father knew little restraint in his language or conduct. When his wife was absent, he focused on Morna, insulting her and even slapping her. The little brother always ran away, but Morna felt she had to stay. She sat in a chair which just fitted the recess formed by a buffet near a corner. Pink china ballerinas graced the buffet, and slender vases with artificial cattails and flowers. Opposite, a discolored antique mirror, reflecting the room askew, seemed a window to a darker reality, where her father's figure truly belonged. With mingled terror and fascination, she watched him in the mirror — but did not find herself there.

Morna remembered numerous repetitions of this scene in a single amalgam.

"What are you looking at, you little shit!" her father had roared. 'What do you see, huh? I'm drunk. I'm a carpenter and a drunk bastard! That ain't good enough for you, I suppose. You're like your mother. Think I'm only here to earn money for you. So you can buy junk. Or throw ten bucks in the preacher's pot. Be a Miss Somebody!" He pranced, mimicking, and stumbled into a chair and gave it an extra kick. A table lamp rocked. "Get out of my way, goddamn it!"

Morna sat very still, moving only her eyes, or adjusting her hands in her lap.

"Moola! That's what you goddamned women want!" he shouted. "But let me go out and spend a nickle on myself, take a little drink like I like to, and I'm a bad sonofabitch. Ba-a-ad sonofabitch! That what your mother tells you behind my back? Huh? She takes you off to church to pray for me, huh? Pray to the blessed Lord to let a house fall on me, huh?" He collapsed onto his knees, pressed palms together and looked at the ceiling. His voice rose in mock supplication, with an effeminate rolling of his head. "Dear God, have mercy upon us and let a house fall on that ba-a-ad sonofabitch! We need his life insurance money to buy rags to drape our asses in and crap to clutter up the house. We need dough for Preacher Bullshit's pot, so he can buy a mink for the heifer that's got him hooked. Give us this day our daily check and forgive us for treating the old man like shit. Lead us into Monkey Ward's and Hinkenbein's and Woolworth's. Deliver us from work. We've **found** the promised land!' That it, huh?" He lumbered to his feet. "That what you do, huh?" He gave a laugh heavy with disgust. "I'm a drunken bastard, and I don't give a shit! And **you** don't give a goddamn about me, you little tramp!" thrusting a finger under her nose. "Don't try to make out different. **You hate my guts!**"

One day not long before Christmas, when Morna was fourteen, he didn't come home. He never came home again. It was the mother's opinion that he had gone to Missouri, where he had relatives, but she did not try to find him. Still, she did not let him be wholly gone. He was the focal point of all their problems. She missed no opportunity to say what he had done to them. Responsibility was hard for her to assume, and she shifted some of it to Morna. On the surface of it, Morna was able to "do her share."

Morna conceived a plan to go and find her father. Had she been a kinder and a better person, he wouldn't have left — so her feelings told her. She would save her money and travel to Missouri and tell him that she loved him. But enactment of the plan lived in some nebulous future time. There was high school to finish, and she mustn't disappoint or offend her mother. At her age, she could not view practically something that was four years in the future. Yet, when high school was over, she still believed in her intention.

During her high school years, she was the kind of angel her mother expected her to be, and she overheard herself praised at the church for having turned out so good after having such a father. One time the minister told her that keeping the commandments was simple. "Only think about doing good things, and you'll only **do** good things. It's a matter of the attitude you have in your head. **Attitude!** All these problems in the world aren't necessary, you know. Happiness is there if people would just reach out and take it."

Morna believed that she believed this. She did not go parking in cars with boys. She smiled a lot, got good grades, was a favorite among her teachers. The real Morna was in her dresser mirror: a quick, symmetrical smile, a clean dress. She was proper remarks, A's on the report card, neat, efficient work at church doings or at Hinkenbein's Department Store, where she worked part time. Moments of anger, sadness or inexplicable pain didn't threaten her, but through the alchemy of adolescent righteousness only intensified her belief in the person others assured her she was. She was a proud achievement — for having had such a father. That thought never confronted honestly the secret liaison her spirit maintained with his.

She worked on at Hinkenbein's, saving her money, unable to know whether or not she would actually go in search of her father, but somehow still consoled by the idea. Then one day a young man bought some shirts from her and stopped a moment to talk. He came back again in two days and asked her to let him buy her lunch. She did. They had another date, and he did not make advances. He had good manners: he did not touch her. She had just broken up with a schoolmate who wanted to marry her. He planned to become a doctor, and was an easy-going, generous fellow, but his casual attitude to sex had made her angry, deeply resentful. Her new friend was not a happy person. His name was Ross Fehler. His father had died recently, and Ross took care of the ranch where the family had lived. The mother was sick and had returned to Aureole. Ross' problems entangled Morna's feelings — she began to try to take responsibilities. Ross came frequently to see her. Very soon, he came with liquor on his breath.

"You've been drinking!" she said. "That won't help anything."

"Yeah!" he snapped. "I suppose that burns you up. Baptist! I haven't got enough things getting at me that I can take a little drink once in a while. I go down in the pasture and find one of my best critters killed by lightning — or maybe someone poisoned her . . ."

"Was there one dead?" She felt repentant.

"Well, there could easily have been. It happens all the time. And I have to look after that place all by myself. Have to look after my mother. But all you can think of is whether I take a little drink. That's the important thing. Jesus Christ!" They were sitting in his pickup. He stared ahead through the windshield, right hand shifting restively over the wheel, face strained.

"I'm sorry," Morna pleaded. "I'm sorry. I didn't mean anything. I know what you're up against."

"**How** do you know? Tell me that. **How** do you know?"

"No, I guess I don't know. I'm sorry. I didn't mean . . . I shouldn't have said anything." Pain at the sense of his pain burst automatically in her.

From then on, concern for her father dimmed. Ross and his problems were immediate. As the relationship developed, his anxiety and misery became an intimate part of her — yet her mind was so much oriented by the idea of public joy in love that she believed herself happy.

They were married in her church, "The little stone church with the warm heart." Marriage, she thought, would put an end to their quarrels. They would **have** each other, and she would show him the way out of his strange trouble. However, the two people she had thought them only privately and transitorily to be, slowly emerged into the light of her mind as their realities.

Also, marriage ended her chastity, which had permitted a detachment and self-possession that buffered her sensibilities. Sexual intercourse violated her spiritual cocoon — although Ross made only a brief physical entrance. She discovered that she had secretly believed sex to be an ultimate expression of love. It did indeed open the way to feelings — but disgust and hatred were among them, no longer tidily rationalized.

Ross approached her once a week, on Saturday nights. He initiated a spirit of silliness, sometimes putting on her panties or bra and clowning. That made her uncomfortable, but she went along, maybe tickling his ribs, giggling with his giggles — both of them acting like children being naughty, until somehow, almost accidentally, they were naked and joined. But he was unwilling to carry the experience beyond his own gratification. When it was over for him, he turned away to repossess himself. A few times she had asked him to help her further, but he had shifted away, grumbling: "For Christ's sake!" Sometimes she went to the bathroom on a pretense of washing herself — ran water, but it didn't work. She could not give herself artificial stimulation. It only increased the congestive ugliness in her body. Next morning, relieved to be over the feelings, she shut that part of her life away and penitentially set about being a good wife — until another weekend brought a repetition.

Ross had said he didn't want children for a while, until he had built up the place. But Morna had a vivid sense of a child with them. She agreed with Ross in good faith, but then she ran out of contraceptive jelly — even forgot to get more in town. When Ross found out, he said: "You didn't tell me you didn't have the stuff."

"I thought you wanted me," she replied. "You seemed to."

He gave an exasperated snort. "It's **my** fault then!"

"Does it **have** to be a fault?"

He sighed and shook his head. They didn't actually quarrel much. But he never spoke to her with his eyes on her. Generally his voice was loud and slurred, and his eyes found all of the room but the part she occupied.

Their lives went on, like an uneasy truce, until one day in the fifth month of her pregnancy Ross came home drunker than she had yet seen him. She was afraid — as she had sometimes been before — but expected only moodiness from him.

He hulked about the living room and pawed through his desk. Finally he asked: "Where the hell's that letter from Hodges?" Hodges was his lawyer.

"I haven't touched it," she said. "I haven't seen it."

"I put it right on this desk."

"I haven't been near it."

"Why can't a man ever find anything in this goddamned house?" He grabbed up a stack of letters and slapped them down again. "You're mighty damned careless with anything that matters to me. I know very well I had that letter right here. Why isn't it here? Did you throw it in the fire? White got that lease I was after. Hodges was supposed to be looking out for me. I want to go back and see what the sonofabitch said in that letter, because I think he's crooked. Now I can't find the letter."

"I never take anything off your desk." She wanted to sit down, but there was no chair at hand.

"But you don't give a damn about it, do you? All you do is piddle around here thinking up ways to spend my money."

Mechanically, irrelevantly, she said: "I don't remember you telling me you were trying to get that land."

"I didn't? I **didn't**? That's fifty goddamned times. Pay attention."

Trying not to react like a little girl, she was angered, humiliated, but could muster only the resolve to say: "I'm not going to argue about it."

She started out of the room. But he sprang after her and spun her against the wall. "Don't walk away from me, goddamn it!"

She strained back, covering herself with her arms. "**Be careful of me**! Be careful for the baby!"

Alcohol had released the violence of powerlessness. "I don't give a **shit** about the baby! I didn't want any kids until I got a place built up. But you . . . It's just another way to foul me up." Then he let go of her and drew back, seeming to get a focus on himself. He turned and left the house.

She was conscious of fear receding in her, and she came close to a feeling of honest hatred. For a little while, she saw them both with a cold clarity; saw them as two petty individuals incapable of rising out of themselves. But that vision was soon lost amid the controlling specifics of her life. Ross didn't apologize when he came in — yet he was soft-spoken. And next day, when he came from town, he made a point of saying two beers was enough. Another day, he admonished her to be careful of the baby.

She entertained no serious thought of leaving him. At a ladies' club meeting she laughed and talked easily about the baby and about Ross' anticipation of a son. Nothing had changed in her words with the ladies. And it was too much for her, to say alone inside herself that something had changed, and that she ought to act accordingly.

In a way, she expected Ross to get drunk and blow up again, but he did not. Perhaps, she thought, he had scared himself sufficiently. He showed restraint — yet he had begun to make uncomplimentary remarks about her in the presence of visitors and then laugh. No one else pretended the remarks were funny. Often he quarreled with her in a controlled way, pretending to discuss.

After Donnie was born, Morna began to say: "Don't wake the

baby!" "You'll upset Donnie." Or she left the room while he was speaking, saying: "I've got to look after the baby."

Alone, Morna turned on the TV to watch variety or quiz shows. Strapping Donnie in his portable seat, she set him to watch, made him laugh, told him — told herself — one day he would appear on the picture tube.

Ross was gone most of the time — if not working, then off to town. Morna talked to her baby. A new dress she sewed was modeled for the mirror and for him; a new cookie recipe was for him, before he was old enough to eat cookies.

She was the good wife again, in a more deliberate way: polite, never raising her voice to Ross, never trying to get back at him — even when he lost his temper after she accidentally backed the pickup into a post, or accidentally dropped a sack of beer bottles he had passed to her, or over-salted his soup, or over-cooked his steak, or broke his favorite screwdriver.

They usually went out Saturdays, to a dance or to visit someone, and he drank enough to make him feel good. Back home then, they performed their weekly sexual anomalism. She tried again to talk to him, asking more time and stimulation before they came together. He chuckled uneasily and said that was what high school kids did in the backseats of cars — was that what she had done?

She had expected such a response — indeed discovered that she welcomed it. For her nerves were braced against intimate emotion now, and it would have been difficult to accept tenderness and fulfillment.

Morna was not unhappy when Ross left in the mornings to work in the fields, or take care of his cattle, or go on one of his many unexplained trips. She knew he usually went to the saloon and brooded or tried to get information about land or cattle. She was relieved to be alone — yet loneliness gave her time for depression and anxiety. Sometimes in the ostensibly tranquil scene of living room and kitchen, she sensed ominous forces: Donnie was going to get sick; Ross would be killed on the road; she would accidentally cut her wrist and be unable to get help. No, she told herself, none of this makes any sense. But the feeling was in the air.

In February, there had been an initial culmination in the dark progress of her life. During a warm spell, Ross had asked Herm McNeil to come over with his forklift and loosen up a haystack and shift it into a lot where it could be easily fed, come a March blizzard. Morna had met McNeil only a few times. He lived across the highway south, but the two families never visited socially.

McNeil was a harelip. He had had an operation, but the scar was prominent, and in a side view his upper lip was flat while the lower one protruded. Front view, the upper lip was asymmetrical, with the pinkish scar slightly left. His hair was an indefinite light brown, combed in coarse strands to one side. His eyes were blue; a strange shallow-water blue. They were keen, perfect — incongruous with his damaged mouth, his self-deprecating jokes and obsequious manners. At first Morna saw the servile, marred expression when he turned her way — later she saw only the eyes.

McNeil kept up a fairly steady banter. He told Ross to go ahead and wash up, but Ross invited him to be first. "Well, I'll just erode the top soil a little," McNeil said. "Don't want to disturb the hardpan." And at the table: "Oh, boy! Fried chicken! Don't get that too often. Old lady sells the meat and serves me the cackle!" Always in an easy, half-nasal drawl. "I must have the poorest land around here. Two jack rabbits starved to death on my east forty last year. My cows are so skinny the kids run sticks down their ribs like slat fences."

Ross grunted a commanding chuckle. "Well, cheer up, Herm. Spring's just around the corner. You'll survive. You'll make it."

"Hell, I don't know," McNeil went on. "I think I'll have to get a government loan to pay my income tax. Maybe I could get them to cancel one out against the other then."

"By God, I think that's the way the big outfits work it!" exclaimed Ross, seeming to possess the whole table with strength and confidence. He said not a word to Morna, but when McNeil complimented the pie, Ross said: "Well, there ought to be something they can do right, you know."

Then he and McNeil got up and went outside, Ross talking rough and loud. Only McNeil turned a last glance back, letting Ross go on ahead of him.

Morna, picking up the dishes, felt a pressure of danger in the room. She did not want to be alone; Ross must come back in. Yet she was secretly aware of an inadmissible excitement.

She heard an engine. Through the window, she could see the pickup leaving and McNeil on his way to the tractor.

Morna did the dishes and changed Donnie and put him down for his nap. Then she stood in the front room, listening for her deepest feelings. Nothing. Only the irregular bellow of the tractor's engine outside, as its governor opened and closed, adjusting the power to the work. Morna lay down and covered her eyes with her wrist. But something was strange and restive inside her. She got up and moved through the room. Her sewing machine was out. She sat down at it. **A time to rend and a time to sew** . . . The work held no interest. Her body was charged with an unfamiliar urgency.

At last she made some coffee and filled a pint jar. Donning a light jacket, she went out toward the barn.

When McNeil saw her, he shifted the tractor out of gear, shoved the throttle to idle and jumped down. "Say, I can sure use that! Just what I needed. How come you read my mind?"

She stood in the sun by the stack, and the air was pleasantly warm. "I just thought you might like a drink."

He gulped from the jar. "I sure do. Nothing beats coffee." His nasal squawk was gentle. He glanced at the stack. "Well, I'm getting her done. If that old tractor holds out. It's so old everything's been replaced but the idea, and that was no good to start with!" His eyes came back, inspecting her. "You look a little chilly."

"I . . . haven't felt too good."

"What's the matter? Weather like this!"

She sighed a little laugh. Then, not being able to think of anything to say, she shrugged.

Before the moment grew too long, he said: "Everyone feels a little down once in a while, I guess. You got a pretty tough row — town girl on a farm."

She felt a little catch of pain in her eyes, and her body went foolishly weak.

She felt him see all this, yet his eyes did not dwell to embarrass her. "You sure do all right though. Don't know when I've eaten such a good meal!" He stepped up, putting out a hand to pat her arm. The hand stayed; he was in her space, closer than her sense of such things allowed. But just as compunction might have drawn her away, he said: "Now you don't want to cry about nothing," and instantly her eyes were flooded. His arm having bridged the physical distance, he now moved in, not bringing the scarred face to hers, but guiding her head over his shoulder. "You just got a little trouble maybe. It'll turn out all right."

She had an intimation of being beyond option now, given over indifferently to a requisite debasement. She felt a nausea not so much of her body as of her spirit. His hands explored quickly, efficiently, denying the irregularity in his touch. She felt out of herself, and her mind could not take hold. Her eyes were on the field, and then the sky, and it was cloudless, without dimensions, without surface — blue, like shallow water, adrift in itself, timeless, passive.

The experience was worse than she might have imagined. Her body had not awakened to him, and even his awkward compensation with spit left his intrusion rough and painful. Her thighs tightened, her body shrank, but he was firm upon her with a power Ross had never shown. Finished, he got to his feet, and she glimpsed a furtive, impersonal satisfaction in his eyes. He did not help her up, and she felt miserably undignified getting her feet under her. Picking up the coffee jar, she started for the house, stumbled and caught herself with one hand. She crossed level ground, yet walked as if climbing a hill in heels. The world was not steady around her.

It seemed to her that the experience ought to belong to her private reality; it should have nothing to do with Ross. Yet, at the door her heart froze: **Ross is home!** But no. **She** had not closed the door tightly — as if her egression were somehow tentative. She went quickly to the bathroom and washed herself and combed her hair — then rushed in sudden panic to look at Donnie. He slept with his thumb in his mouth. She leaned against the doorjamb, sighing deep breaths. In the bathroom again, she took off her dress and shook a few stems of hay from it — telltale bits charged with significance. She stuffed the dress into a hamper under other clothes.

Ross would ask: **Why did you change your dress?**

Donnie spat up on it.

He would go to the hamper, find the dress, pick bits of hay from it — discover a spot on the lower back, but none on the front.

Morna dug out the dress and went over it inch by inch. There was no spot, no hay any more. It looked all right to wear. She pushed it deep into the hamper again.

The pickup rattled in the yard, and Morna sprang out of the bathroom — but it was only the tractor echoing against the barn.

Another bolt: McNeil would tell! He and Ross had made it up between them to show her up. They would come in together wearing savage, disgusted smiles, and they would take Donnie away. She would be put in jail. A movie image of a cell block flashed through her mind — then another image of Susan Hayward in the gas chamber.

When Ross did come home, Morna's heart felt monstrous and labored heavily. He scarcely looked at her. She felt he should be able to read in her face what had happened. But when he settled in a chair with the newspaper, fear in her resolved itself into a strange impulsion. She walked about the room, back and forth in front of him, doing seriously things that were utterly trivial — straightening a doily; then returning to adjust it again.

Ross was deep in his paper.

Morna set up the ironing board. Then she got the iron and plugged it in. She took some of Donnie's clothes from a closet — went to the hamper and dug out her dress. Busily she ironed these items, at a knife-point of expectancy.

Ross threw the paper aside and got up. "Going out to see what that damned McNeil did with the hay," he said. McNeil had left earlier.

Morna unplugged the iron and hung the dress in the bedroom doorway. She felt in curious uneasy balance between a specious elation and serious depression. Nothing she could imagine would dispel these feelings.

Ross stayed out until suppertime. By then, Morna had taken a large swallow of cough medicine for the codeine. A dull sense of unreality possessed her. Fact and imagination were not sharply distinct, and the world seemed bearable. She felt less confined by time and physicality. There was a mystery into which she wished to go deeper, but night and the morning brought her back. Morning was cluttered with facts she did not like but could not now change. They seemed building blocks in an inevitable structure, unless she by some force of will was able to change their meaning. She saw this clearly, yet outwardly there was nothing to decide — nothing to do but wait. **I should not have married Ross,** she thought. But now there was Donnie. He slept, laughed, nursed his bottle — still hung onto that old bottle! She focused upon him to infuse what was required of her. At the same time, she entered a little into his world to leave her own. Yet behind this, as the days and weeks went on, she was waiting, and she knew it. It was scarcely a fact for the light of day — what nonsense! Then tears over some little thing would strip away the veil. So it went.

Now, sorting over these matters again, she gazed absently through the kitchen window above the sink. A sudden sharp flash of light struck her eyes. Then she saw that someone was riding out in the neighbor's pasture to the north. He was on a white horse, angling across her line of vision at a canter. She watched until he disappeared behind the barn. Then another movement caught her eye. There was a rabbit feeding on new shoots just north of the yard fence. He crept along nipping and sitting back to look around. His ears lay along his shoulders, now and then switched forward to listen. He was so much the color of dead weeds and earth that he could disappear in the slightest growth. Morna watched and began to feel that she wanted to go out. She wanted to touch the rabbit. He looked soft and clean and very much at peace with the world.

She took a sugar cube from the cabinet. Then she hesitated, put it back and got some lettuce from the refrigerator. Slipping on her jacket, she went out, located the rabbit again and approached slowly. It froze. Morna spoke to it: "Here, little bunny. Look what I've got for you. Come on and take it. It's real good. Nice juicy lettuce!"

But the rabbit bolted; vanished round the barn. Morna followed. Not finding it, she went on, through a row of trees. There were weeds and thistles here and there. She walked up and down, looking among them.

A horse cleared its nose with a quick blast, and she looked up to find the rider she had just seen across the fence from her. His horse was not really white — it was gray. She could see nothing that might have made the flash — except the rider's glasses. He got down, grinning and hunching his shoulders a little. He was very good-looking.

"Hello. Lose something maybe?"

"Hi," she said, and a prickle of uneasiness went through her.

"What you looking for?" he persisted.

"A rabbit!" she heard herself give a foolish little laugh.

"Putting salt on his tail?" Grinning wider than ever, he hooked his thumbs in his belt.

"Salt?"

"That's the way you catch them."

"Really?" She scarcely paid attention to the banter. Her breath came heavily with the compelling stimulus of danger.

"Sure," he kept on a bit awkwardly. "Didn't you know that's all you have to do?"

In side vision, as she kicked through the weeds, she could see him looking up and down her body. "I think someone's trying to kid someone."

"Now why would I want to kid you?"

Her eyes skirted the haystacks. Then she stopped and looked straight at him. He was perhaps six feet tall, with sandy-brown hair and brown eyes — a hat pushed back on his head. She met his gaze. "You didn't see my rabbit?"

"No, I didn't. But I sure wish I had some salt . . ."

His eyes dropped to her breasts, and she crossed her arms in front of her. "I have a little boy," she said all 'at once. "Did you know I've got a little boy?"

He shook his head slightly. "Maybe that rabbit hid in among them haystacks, huh?"

"I've got to go tend to my little boy."

"I could help you find that rabbit."

Her heart pounded. Emotion burst vertiginously. She knew what was going to happen and began laughing.

"What's the joke?"

"You!" she cried. "You're the joke!" Turning, she ran back to the house.

Donnie was at the bars of his play pen. He grinned and stamped, cooing nonsense words. She picked him up and pressed him close, very, very close, laughing into his play clothes until her laughter turned to tears.

The Old Woman Who Read to Her House Plants

Five years since he had been back to the town. It had been shrinking for fifty years, but now even such basic features as the depot and the grain elevator were gone. The post office survived, and a filling station, a saloon, a hotel. All separated by vacant lots — as many as three in a row. You could see through the studs of the restaurant, and the church had collapsed.

Len Schneider was pushing forty. He had left the farm-ranch country of the prairies to become an English professor on the West Coast. Freed of his classes and freshly divorced, he was back for the summer. In the car beside him was Sheila, nineteen, a guest on a ranch next to his dad's old place. His dad was dead; his mother lived in the city an hour's drive away. Len stayed with her. They got along all right, but he had been glad to put half the country between him and his dad. He had put every kind of distance between them: education, work, character. Character most of all, he believed. His parents' marriage had been hell, but they had lacked the courage for a divorce. Len, on the other hand, had made a clean break.

Now, here was Sheila beside him. Supposedly, he was just giving her a ride. They were delivering a bag of wheat to old Mrs. Kobelsky who used it in making bean-bag frogs. Yet he had dropped by the ranch where Sheila stayed several times already — visiting with the Joneses, whom he had known since childhood. His fantasies had begun to build a courtship. Why not? He was free, successful, a professional person. The Joneses might not like it, of course — attitudes about age differences and so forth didn't change around here. But he was no longer of their world — his dad's world. His dad had liked **Playboy** calendars. Paper girls were safe and easy to come by. He had been a lion at home and a lamb in the world. Len felt a comfortable satisfaction in that distinction also.

"Town's drying up," he said.

"All these little towns seem to be dwindling." Her words were too carefully chosen. She was trying to be older. Twenty-one!

He drove down Main Street. The old grocery store was closed, the last false-fronted building that recalled the original town. There had been half a dozen when he attended high school. The high school too was gone. He caught a breath to tell her how it had been, but checked himself because she hadn't yet been born then.

"Where does Mrs. Kobelsky live?"

"Over here." She pointed off to the right. He could see a few houses across the block. "Do you know her?"

He nodded. "I knew them when they were on the farm. Out by Joneses, you know?"

"Yes. Brice showed me."

"How is Leroy?"

"Well! He's the same as always, I guess."

There was a double note in her voice because Leroy Kobelsky was mentally defective. Len did not know just how the doctors classified him, but he could not talk or control his movements well and was confined to a wheelchair. He was slightly younger than Len.

"She must have quite a problem with him these days," said Len. He turned a corner and drove the long way around toward Mrs. Kobelsky's house.

"Since her husband died, I guess she's had some worry. She's such a little thing."

"That's what I meant."

"She does so marvelously though. She's so marvelous."

"Yes," he said. "Gentle. She's got something in her that keeps her going."

"She sure has!"

Amid the relics of the town, Nattie Kobelsky's yard bloomed with zinnias, four-o'clocks, roses and trellises of ivy. It was a dinky place, struggling to stay a respectable white beside the unpaved street. The remains of a sidewalk ran before it — poor cement deteriorated into half-buried lumps of hardened gravel like something Roman. A picket fence stood tenuous guard along the front; cheap snow fence completed the encirclement. A little gate stood open. Len, brightened, animated by his sprightly companion, almost tripped along the walkway. Sheila was ahead; he let her be in charge.

She raised a hand but hesitated before knocking. There was a mumble of conversation within the house. She touched a finger across her lips. He listened. It was not a conversation; not an exchange. Being very quiet, he could pick it up.

" . . . so she said nothing. 'Seven years and six months!' Humpty Dumpty repeated thoughtfully. 'An uncomfortable sort of age. Now if you'd asked **my** advice, I'd have said 'Leave off at seven' — but it's too late now.' 'I never ask advice about growing,' Alice said indignantly."

Sheila's cheeks puffed with a trapped giggle.

Alice, Athena! Len thought, looking at her. His hand rose involuntarily, but he refrained from touching her.

" 'Too proud?' the other enquired. Alice felt even more indignant at this suggestion. 'I mean,' she said . . .''

Sheila stole to a window at the edge of the stoop and peered in. She tip-toed back; stifled another giggle. She was so close he could brush her hair with his lips, smell a faint perfume, see the swell of a small breast down the low-cut neck. She made a little rap on the door.

In half a minute, it opened. Len saw that Nattie Kobelsky had aged a good deal. She had always been small, but now she seemed a mere wisp of a person. Already in opening the door, she was aquiver with bashful pleasure. Yet even the pleasure seemed to awaken a force of sadness in her. The corners of her mouth smiled down, not up, and her teeth played over her lower lip uncertainly.

"Well!" she exclaimed, and then it seemed difficult for her to find more words. She stood back, while Len and Sheila, jumbling their greetings together, stepped inside.

Nattie found her voice again: "Len Schneider! Been years!" Her speech, like the childish squirm of her body, was muffled, apparently in acute self-consciousness.

Sheila had the bag of wheat. She presented it ceremoniously like frankincense. "The wheat! For the frogs!"

"Oh! Heavens!" Nattie took it, squeezing it in her hands as if to betoken appreciation. Then she dropped it at a door left of the entrance. Her bedroom, Len guessed.

The house smelled of baking. And if the yard was a modest flower festival, the cramped living room was a jungle: great philodendrons, elephant's-ears, jade plants, cactuses — Len couldn't have named everything. Leroy, in his wheelchair near the window, gurgled and stuck out his hand. Len shook it. His head jerked to one side, and his jaw made a circle. But had he been in physical control, he would have been quite an ordinary-looking man — young for his age.

"Won't you sit down?" Nattie invited.

They sat — Sheila, inadvertently, near the wheelchair. Len tensed, for Leroy groped toward her. She was out of reach.

Mrs. Kobelsky was saying: "Len, when did you get back? How long you going to stay for?"

Distracted, he answered her so briefly that there was a moment of silence.

Sheila broke it: "I love that book!" **Through the Looking-Glass** was open face-down on a lamp table.

Mrs. Kobelsky gave a little jump as if she had been caught in an oversight. "Oh! Yes. I like it too. I was reading it aloud." A smothered chuckle. "The plants are supposed to do better if you sing to them, but I don't sing! Silly!"

"Certainly not!" cried Sheila. "I **know** plants have feelings. They've done experiments. I've heard about them. They **do** do better if you read to them. They're **beautiful!** I've never seen such beautiful house plants." She turned to a potted blue flower on a stand next to Leroy. "What's this one?"

"Oh, that's just an African violet. A wedgewood."

"It's gorgeous! I know if I were a . . ." Her eyes searched about. "A cactus! I'd want to have **Through the Looking-Glass** read to me!"

"You're hardly a cactus," Len put in. "You're . . . orchidaceous."

"What **would** I be as a plant?" She cocked her head.

"A rose!" Nattie suggested, again with a smothered giggle. She pressed into the corner of her chair.

"No thorns!" said Len. "An African violet?"

"An apple tree!" An odd snicker burst from her.

"In blossom!" said Len. The quality of her laugh stayed with him. Her summer skirt was high on her thighs, and she wore no panty hose. He kept his eyes elsewhere.

"And what are you?" she asked him. "A pine? A cedar?"

"Yes. And when you cut me down, there's an empty space against the sky!"

"I know that poem! It's . . . I learned it in school."

"I know it too," said Nattie, and there was a touch of rapport in the air.

Len waited a moment — during which Leroy bellowed softly — and then triumphed over the women: "Markham."

"Markham!" they repeated together.

His mind caught up in the game, Len tried to think what Nattie was — a lily pad for her bean-bag frogs! Yes, most of her under the surface. And Leroy? The gnarled brush that snatches at Snow White fleeing through the forest. His eyes had fallen on a small shelf of books: **Snow White, The Wind in the Willows, Pinocchio,** and several titles that were worn too badly to be read.

Mrs. Kobelsky jumped to her feet. "I'll put the coffee pot on."

"Don't go to any trouble for us," Sheila told her.

"No trouble! I just made some cookies. You're certainly going to have some of my cookies."

"We can't turn that down!" said Sheila. "I'll help." She slipped with Nattie into the kitchen.

Len looked at Leroy. Leroy looked at Len and gurgled mucus in his throat. Len's mind skirted images of caring for Leroy. Thirty-some years, every day, she's got him up, put him to bed, fed him — maybe even kept diapers on him! Did he have sexual impulses? Did he grope at her as she put him to bed? Imagining the old woman handling Leroy, Len conceived that there must be a tough side to her that did not show through her shyness — and perhaps it was that harsher self, not sadness, that shaped her smile. What did she think of **him** with Sheila? He pictured Sheila's body. Girls in his classes wore skirts so short he could sometimes see the crotch of their panty hose while lecturing.

On an impulse, he half rose to get **Through the Looking-Glass** from its table. Because it was open, the place Nattie had been reading was not hard to find. " 'What a beautiful belt you've got on!' Alice suddenly remarked," Len read softly aloud. "(They had had quite enough of the subject of age, she thought: and, if they really were to take turns in choosing subjects, it was her turn now.)"

Sheila, at the kitchen door, asked: "Are they listening?"

He sent her a smile. "Well, the elephant's-ears are!"

"Come out and see the crocuses and Dolly Dimples."

"Really?"

His mock astonishment at the latter name brought a pleased titter from her.

In her kitchen, he discovered that Dolly Dimples are a type of miniature African violet. Nattie had them lined along the window. "They're easy to grow," she explained, "and that kind don't take up much room." She was munching a cookie. The last batch was still on the table where it had been turned out to cool.

Through the back window, Len could see tulips and flags, and something he thought were hollyhocks. His mother used to raise some of these flowers when she was on the ranch. Susan, his ex-wife, had had flowers in town. **Black-eyed Susans**, he thought ironically. He had hit her once, when she was being especially exasperating. She had made a science of being exasperating. Anything to get at him. "There **is** a male menopause," she would say, given any opportunity: his glance at another woman; his fussing in the house. She knew how to bring out the beast.

"I just **love** this kitchen!" said Sheila.

Len turned back. The room was half in dark-brown stain, half in ivory, with stained trim at the windows. It looked nice, but he noticed that the linoleum, under recent paint, was badly worn — and the floor sloped toward one corner. It wasn't much of a house, but she had put a good face on what she had.

The coffee pot began to perk.

Sheila went on about how conveniently arranged the kitchen was. At the far end was a utility room, partly closed off by a long, collapsible door. Len could see an iron bed, with bars on the side away from the wall. Under some carelessly hung clothes, a heavy chair showed — an over-sized potty chair, he thought.

"Have a cookie! Have a cookie!" Mrs. Kobelsky invited, almost ordered.

"My favorite!" said Len, taking one. They were chocolate chip. Nattie helped herself to another one.

Len sat at the table, picking a chair from which he could not see Leroy.

Nattie got "real cream" from the fridge — brought in by a former neighbor on the farm, she said. One of the little things she enjoyed and might as well have.

Sheila sat across from Len. He gave her a little smile, his eyes flirting over her neckline. The dress, a blue-on-white print, had broad, buttoned straps over the shoulders. Apparently one button was missing, and she had substituted a silver brooch very effectively. His eyes on it drew Sheila's down momentarily.

In side vision, he saw Mrs. Kobelsky freeze for an instant. He caught himself shifting uneasily. Deliberately then, he looked right at the old woman, but there were so many nervous visitations on her face that her thoughts were not discernible. She kept reaching out to the handle of the coffee pot, as if afraid that having to wait might offend them. Because she was eager to please, he did not want to arouse her disapproval.

"Do you sell the bean-bag frogs?" he asked, to get her talking about herself.

"Some." She jerked with a little shrug. "Most, I just give them away. You want one?"

"Well, I didn't mean to ask for one . . ."

Out she went immediately, through the living room, and returned with a green frog the size of a barret. She dropped it on the corner of the table and poked it toward Len.

"It's **beautiful**!" said Sheila.

"Can we pay for it?" asked Len.

"Heavens no! You brought me the wheat. I should pay **you** for that!"

"Not at all!" cried Sheila.

Mrs. Kobelsky reached abruptly and snapped a loose string from the frog's seam with a gesture so sharp and deft that it startled Len. Then, with the same unfaltering efficiency, she popped two cups onto the table and filled them with coffee.

Len added cream and set the pitcher toward Sheila.

"Where's yours?" Sheila asked the old woman.

She shook her head, and adversity took over her face with the suddenness of a light switch. "Doctor won't let me drink it. Doctor won't let me drink it." She gave them each a portentous glance. "Heart. Arteries. Oh!" She sat in a chair, pressing against the **back of it.**

"They control that pretty well with medication," Len said.

"Gave me some pills!" she flung out a hand scornfully. "What good are pills for me? What good are pills? I'm seventy years old. Something could happen anytime. What would become of **him** then? Who would look after him?"

Len's glance met Sheila's. Her face was pinched with youthful gravity.

"You have relatives, don't you?" Len ventured.

"What relatives? What relatives? He's my only child, and my sister's dead, and you won't get nothing out of **her** children. Karl's folks? You won't get nothing out of them. Besides they're all in California."

"There must be homes . . ." This was dangerous ground, but he felt under pressure from Sheila's eyes.

"Homes!" she snorted. "There's nothing. Nothing." Contradictorily, she added: "Would I let them have him? Do you think I don't know what that State place is? A barn for animals, that's what it is. What do they care for him? What do they know about his needs and his dislikes? He can't stand to have his feet cold. And he only drinks warm milk. He likes to sit in the sun." Her hands fluttered over each other — yet in the midst of her agitation she snatched up a fly swatter and cracked a fly on the stove so fiercely that Len bounced. Nattie went right on: "He won't eat some things. Can't stand greens."

Len hadn't thought of Leroy's having idiosyncracies; he was just a pretend person. Now imagination took him inside the defective body. Maybe Leroy was a normal spirit trapped in a faulty machine. Len had some sense of what that might be like: trying to ski for the first and last time. Or, on the mental side, trying to stay rational with Susan. Now, trying to explain his intentions with Sheila.

Nattie kept on talking: "He **has** learned over the years. I can see it. I can see it. He does crafts. He **did**, when he was able to get some help. Mrs. Williams had a kiln for a while. She did ceramics. She taught him how to do some things. Have you seen what he's done?"

"No!" cried Sheila. "I want to."

Nattie scampered out. Sheila turned to Len. "The poor thing!"

He nodded. He felt a satisfactory welling of compassion, but there was a nibble of hunger in his belly too, and he eyed the cookies. No. Fattening. His dad would have helped himself to several more. Pacifiers. He weighed two and a quarter when he was forty. Len weighed one sixty. His dad had loved sweets, but not people. Thirty years ago he'd said about the Kobelsky's: "Damned fools, they're going to end up in a fix. Why don't they put that kid away some place? What they going to do when they get along in years?" He'd have blown his top now: "Goddamned old heifer! What's the matter with her? Blubbering all over the place about that hulk. Why didn't she put him away years ago?" Women were always "heifers" in his remarks.

Mrs. Kobelsky returned with an armful of objects, which she arranged on the table between Len and Sheila. Two were recognizable as ashtrays; the others she identified as paperweights. All were glazed in bright colors: green, blue, yellow. All of them were little more than blobs, the paperweights fistfuls of mud, the ashtrays fistfuls of mud that had been smacked by the heel of the hand.

"Mrs. Williams called them abstract forms," said Nattie. "She said that's what they're doing in art these days."

Len could hear Leroy gurgling and grunting in the front room. He touched the objects gingerly.

"They're good!" said Sheila. "We did things like this in high school."

Len glanced at her. She was engrossed, turning a blob in her hands.

Nattie said: "He put the glaze on too."

Len had images of Leroy splashing colors on the clay — on himself, Nattie, the floor. He touched a yellow ashtray: "I like that."

"Take it!" She set it closer to him. "If they would just help a little, he could take care of himself. He could sell to the tourists. Why, them shops along the interstate highway make money hand over fist in the summer."

"Tourists buy anything!" said Sheila ingenuously.

But Nattie didn't stumble: "Certainly they do! Why, anything that's locally made, they'll buy. I know it for a fact!"

Len pictured a stand with piles of unsold blobs on the counter, a hefty nurse tending Leroy, who thumped his wet clay. **What, did the hand then of the potter shake**? No one would stop. No one would buy. But then, on the other hand, why not? He wouldn't be the first idiot to get rich selling nothing.

"Why didn't they do that?" Nattie asked. "Why don't the government help him support himself? He'd have to be looked after, but he could still pay his way. And that's the thing they harp about. It wouldn't be putting him in one of them homes. Them terrible places. He would have people coming all the time, and he likes that."

Len nodded.

"All that government money!" she went on. "All them billions! They spend it on slackers and Indians like it was going out of style, but a person that needs some help to help himself, where's he?"

"Do they maybe have craft shops for the handicapped?" Len asked.

She flung up her hands. "Nothing! Nothing! No one. Oh, there's a place for people who can't use their legs, or something like that. But they won't help **him**. There's no place that'll help him."

Leroy was making a fuss in the front room.

"He wants us in there," she said. "He likes to have people around."

"Maybe we should go in then," said Sheila.

"Well, have another cookie first."

They said no thanks, but Nattie, somehow guiltily, slipped one in her mouth.

Len got up. If he stayed standing, he thought, they could prob- ably leave.

They went into the front room. Leroy bobbed and bellowed, ob- viously pleased.

"I suppose we should go," said Len.

Sheila nodded.

"Don't rush off," said Nattie.

Leroy flung an arm toward Sheila and worked his jaw, his grunts becoming repetitive.

"He sees your pin," Nattie told her.

"Oh!" Sheila stepped beside Leroy, bending her shoulder to him slightly.

Leroy's hand, with one ill-guided swipe, caught not the brooch, but the straps of dress and bra together, popping the brooch off and leaving a small, white breast exposed. Sheila stifled an outcry with her hand.

Like a cat the old woman was on top of Leroy: **smack! smack!** to either side of his head — vicious blows that left him reeling and jolted Len with the force of a shorted lightcord. Just as quickly, she fell back, once more the mouse ashiver in its corner.

Sheila's bra had quickly snapped back, and she plucked up the pin to redo the dress. Pink-faced, she glanced at Len with her apple-tree snicker.

But Leroy was mad. Bellowing and flailing, he caught the African violet by the window and sent it, stand and all, crashing to the floor.

Nattie blurted out an anomalous titter and righted the plant, scrap- ing up as much dirt as she could. "Behave!" she barked at Leroy, her tone an interweaving of threat and apology. She tried to help with the brooch. "He reaches for shiny things. You have to be a little bit careful." Her hands trembled, and Sheila had to fasten the pin.

"He didn't hurt anything," said Sheila.

Len urged: "I guess we'd better be on our way."

He couldn't make the remark sound unrelated to what had hap- pened, and Nattie responded faintly: "Oh, really? Well, don't for- get your frog. And your other things." She skittered to the kitchen and returned with them.

They thanked her several times for the coffee and cookies, and each time she thanked them in return for the wheat. Then they were back in the car and quiet for a few moments while they got started. Sheila set the frog above the dashboard. Its head crumpled in, so that the button eyes looked at each other.

Len found his heart still thudding, but he couldn't distinguish the effect of the violence from the effect of Sheila's exposure. And she was strangely calm.

"Poor Nattie!" said Sheila. "Poor Leroy." Wisely, she added: "She reads to **him**, not the plants, you know."

"Of course!" Len was gruffly authoritative. "She thinks he's a little boy who's going to grow up finally. It's part of the fantasy; that and the so-called crafts. That's one side . . ."

"What do you mean? What's the other?"

"You saw."

She fell silent, studying.

He still felt the nibble of hunger, and he imagined Nattie back in the kitchen by now. Guzzling the rest of the coffee! She kept it on hand; she must drink it. Except with company. Then it was a lead in; a way to get to talk about her problem. She kept cream. She was knocking cookies back like salted peanuts. Someone worried about her heart wouldn't be eating cream and sweets. She wasn't fat — yet she probably lived on sweets. And coffee. Justified herself by dumping the grounds on her plants. Good for them!

"But she **does** have a problem!" said Sheila, rather intensely. "What's she going to **do**? What's going to become of him?"

"I couldn't tell you."

"We should do something. We've got to help her. We've got to figure something out."

"She created the predicament. She can't get along with her relatives, and she rejects the homes."

"But there must be something!" Her eyes burned on him.

"Yes." Take care of him ourselves! He was afraid she might land on that. He couldn't take care of Leroy if he wanted to, and his mother wouldn't. That was that. A bolt of anger went through his brain. Selfish old bitch! Why had she let herself get into this mess? It **was** selfishness. But he probably didn't dare explain that to Sheila.

"When a problem's in front of you, you've **got** to do something about it," she was saying. "I believe that. What good is religion? What good is **anything** if you don't live up to it? We know about this problem. So it's **our** problem."

"Some problems people have to work out for themselves."

"Oh, do you believe that? I don't believe that. What's she going to **do**?"

Her skirt had worked up in the car seat, exposing her bare legs. He drew slightly away from her.

"I'm going to talk to Sybil about it." Sybil was Mrs. Jones.

"That's a good idea," he said with a sarcasm so controlled she did not detect it. At least she gave no sign.

He dropped her at the Joneses' gate. "Have to hurry," he said. "I wish you could come in. I wish you could talk to Sybil."

He gave her a little smile and shook his head. "Good-bye."

As she ran down the lane, he turned a wistful, relieved glance after her. Then he drove away.

She had left the frog and both "artifacts" in the car. The latter he pitched into some bushes along the road. The frog, he gave to his mother.

For a week or so, he thought about what had happened — even argued with some imaginary figure as he might with a student over a story. It balanced out, didn't it? If he wasn't doing anything about Nattie, well, he had given up his young girl. It was a kind of moral quid pro quo. Wasn't it?

Winter
Wheat

Bud was eleven and his Uncle Art had promised to let him drive the pickup when the custom combiners arrived. They would have a truck and Uncle Art would let them haul the wheat directly to the elevator in Pinnacle. Bud would drive the half-ton pickup and haul what it held to Uncle Art's granary. It was the first summer that Bud would get to work with the combiners. They had self-propelled machines — Massey-Harris, Farmall, International. They came from Texas, and they followed the harvest north, way up into Canada. One day they appeared and when the fields were cut, they were gone. Bud had tried to imagine their journeys; what kind of roads they went down and what kind of country they saw. But it was hard for him, because he had never been outside South Dakota. He had always lived on his dad's farm.

His dad did not plant wheat. He said this was not wheat country. He planted cane and millet to feed the sheep. Bud often had to herd the sheep in order to keep them on a rented pasture his dad didn't want to fence. While herding, Bud watched the trucks on the highway and the tractors in neighboring fields. During harvest time, he watched the combines and thrashing rigs. Finally, this summer, his Uncle Art had asked his dad if Bud could drive the pickup for him. His dad had consented, but at home he said: "He's looking for some free help. I don't know that he's ever come down here and given me a hand with anything." He told Bud: "You ought to ask him how much he's going to pay you." Then he gave a little laugh which Bud knew had nothing to do with things being funny, although Bud always smiled at his dad when his dad gave that laugh. But he did not ask Uncle Art how much he was going to get paid. For what if Uncle Art should change his mind?

It was hard to do nothing but herd the sheep while he waited for the day the combines would arrive. He stuck a lath into the ground and put a dead thistle on top of it and sat in the shade — it was terribly hot — and dreamt. His uncle would introduce him: "This is Bud. He drives the pickup." He would shake hands with the man who drove the big self-propelled combine and with the man who drove the truck. Maybe the combine would break down. And he would be the one to fix it. "It's this chain here. We'll fix it with my belt buckle. Just fits!" Or the grasshoppers would be moving in like an army and he would say: "Cut in front of them. Don't go around the field. They move too fast. Got to go back and forth in front of them." And the wheat would be saved.

When the combiners came, his mother would have to watch the sheep or put them in a fenced pasture. He would be doing the important thing, and she would be looking after his chore. "How long do you think it will be before they get here?" he asked her.

"Oh, four, five days," she told him. "Don't get excited. They'll come when they come."

And his dad said: "If that damned Art had bound that grain he would have it all down now. With this heat we're liable to get hail. He don't know nothing. If he was smart he wouldn't even plant wheat. He'd get a bunch of sheep and plant some cane."

Bud knew what Uncle Art would have answered. "Bind, hell! Then you go around the country thrashing for a month. I want the stuff combined. One day, that's it."

Bud was glad. There was nothing as wonderful as a self-propelled combine. Someday he would own one somehow. He would drive it. Maybe he would be a custom combiner, or maybe he would plant his own big fields of wheat.

When, three days later, Bud saw a truck on a side road hauling a self-propelled combine, he left the sheep and ran almost half a mile to tell his mother. "The combiners are here! I saw them!"

"Well, they're going to Stinson's first. Then they have a half a day at Haug's. Don't get in a rush. You better hustle back there and watch them sheep."

It seemed twice as hot walking back to the sheep as it had seemed running to the house. In the afternoon, Bud watched thunderheads poking up in the west. He wished they would come over the sun so that it would cool. But then he thought about what his dad had said about hail. "Don't hail. Don't hail," he said to the sky. Later he could hear the thunder and see the lightening in the distance, but the clouds never covered the sun.

Two days later, Uncle Art came over at dinner time — he was a bachelor and liked to stop in at dinner time. He was a small man, and very thin and bony. "Them combiners are broke down over at Haug's," he said. "Looks like they ain't going to get to my wheat tomorrow after all."

Bud's dad said, "You should have bound that wheat. You can't depend on other people.

Uncle Art said: "Well, a man's binder could break down too. Anyway, next year I'm going to have me a combine. It's a good crop this year. I'll get me one of them little self-propels, and Bud can drive the pickup. We'll do her ourselves."

Bud sat up straight and twisted a little in his seat and grinned.

"Oh, that's damn foolish," his dad said. "You don't get one crop in three years. The damned machine will just set around and rust." Uncle Art, having no family, had always spent his money on machinery. His farm was cluttered with rusted-out machines he had bought new but used very little.

Bud said, "Maybe we could go out custom combining."

Uncle Art said: "I thought of that. If I could make enough money, I'd buy another section. Then I'd get a big combine and a big truck. How'd you like that, Bud?"

"I could learn to drive the combine when I get a little older," Bud said.

His uncle nodded.

"Ten years ago you was going to buy another eighty," said Bud's dad. "You ain't been able to buy one acre in ten years, so how do you figure on buying another section next year?"

"I only need one good crop," said Uncle Art. "I'm going to have a good crop this year, and I bet I'll have one next year."

Uncle Art left, saying he would come back to get Bud when the combiners arrived.

Bud could hardly sleep that night. Next day he kept watching for Uncle Art to come down the road. At noon he drove the sheep to the water hole and went in to eat. He asked his mother whether Uncle Art had been there. Why hadn't the combiners fixed the combine yet? When would they come?

"Keep your shirt on," his mother told him. "They'll come."

That day passed and then the next. The day after that it hailed. Bud had driven the sheep in as the storm approached. He watched with his mother and dad as the hail stones beat the house and the lone apple tree and the hollyhocks. "Damn good thing that I got a lot of feed left from last year," his dad said.

After the storm, his dad drove with him to Uncle Art's. They didn't know whether the hail had struck Art's field or not. But they found out that it had. The tall wheat was broken down to a wet hash.

His dad looked over the field and shook his head. "Damn fool!" he said. "If he'd bound that grain he'd have it now. You see? You see how he is? He fools around with them combiners and this is what he gets."

Then they went up to the house, where they found Uncle Art tinkering with a part from the engine of his pickup. "Well, that was some storm, wasn't it?" he remarked, grinning.

"Did you see what it did to your wheatfield?" Bud's father asked.

"I ain't been out there yet," said Uncle Art. "Had a little trouble starting the pickup and thought I better try and get the bugs out of it before the combiners came."

"Well, you won't have to worry about that anymore," said Bud's dad. "Come on. Get in my car. I'll drive you out."

The three of them drove back to the field. They got out and walked through the battered wheat.

Bud's dad said: "What have I always been telling you? This is no country for trying to make your living off grain. Get some sheep. They're the thing."

"Hell," said Uncle Art, "I don't want no damn sheep. You have to lamb them and shear them and dip them and feed them. Baby them all year around. Walk through their manure."

"You afraid of work?" asked Bud's dad. "I sure don't see you making no fortune this way."

Uncle Art walked on. Bud's dad followed, and Bud trailed behind. He didn't want them to look at him. He didn't want them to see his eyes.

Uncle Art stopped walking and stood with his hands on his hips, the thumbs forward, the fingers on his back. He stood very still, with his head cocked ever so slightly to the right, and he looked across the field for quite a long time. Bud and his dad stood nearby and looked at him.

Finally Art spoke to them. "This fall I'm going to put in winter wheat. Winter wheat matures earlier. Next year I'll have a good crop and get it out of the field early. Then if I can get me some more land and a combine, I can raise a bigger crop the year after. Keep on building up like that. Winter wheat's the thing. I should have planted it for years. I'm going to start getting the tractor in shape right now. Then I'll see about a loan for some seed. I'll plow this stuff under and keep the ground worked up so the weeds don't get a start. Come fall I'll be ready to put her in to winter wheat."

On the way home, Bud's dad kept shaking his head and muttering: "Goddamnfool! I've never seen the beat!"

Next day Bud was out with the sheep. He stuck a lath in the ground and put a thistle on it and sat in the shade. Across the prairie, rippling in the sun, he pictured endless fields of winter wheat. And into it he drove with a great red combine. Massey-Harris, Farmall, International — it bore one of those magic names. It moved along like the electric clipper on the back of his neck when he went to the barber shop, and it sheared the prairie of thousands of bushels of wheat.

The Burial of the Bride

Claude had met her in front of the saloon in the little town of Pinnacle one night when he was partly drunk. Her family lived in a tent outside the town, beyond the stockyards, where the Indians always camped. She had walked up town because her father was drunk, she told him. Her name was Mary.

He had joked with her, expecting her to run away or ignore him. Instead she had giggled. That excited him, and he went up close to her. He talked some more and then started putting his hands on her, and the sensation of touch sharpened his appetite for touch, until he had her backed up against the saloon, pressing his body on hers and fondling her. She got in his car when asked, and they drove down the road. Claude looked for a place to park, but kept going until they were at his shack on the north range of the Fleming ranch. She went in with him, but there, in privacy, everything changed. He became afraid and responsible and treated her politely, keeping his hands off her. They became quite tender with each other and had something to eat. Finally, they slept together in their clothes on the bed. The shack had two small rooms.

Next day, her father came. "You take my girl!" he cried, short, fat, big-nosed, dressed in boots, Levi's, a bright red shirt and a ten-gallon hat. "You can't take my girl! First you give me ten dollars for whiskey. Then, take her. Give me ten dollar. Whiskey! Ten dollar! Whiskey!"

Claude was scared about bringing the girl home, for she looked under twenty-one. He gave the Indian ten dollars, and the Indian drove off in his broken-down Model A.

For a while, Claude wished he had sent the girl away and saved the money. Sober now, he scarcely knew how to talk to her or what to do with her. But he had paid ten dollars and, thinking it over, began to feel she was in some way his. Her idleness made him feel angry. Drawing himself up, he ordered: 'Wash the dishes!"

She washed the dishes.

Claude looked about the room. "Sweep the floor!"

She swept the floor. Then she began picking up his clothes and junk scattered about the room. That made him feel guilty, and he started helping. They reached for an old shirt on a chair at the same time. Both drew back, deferring to the other. They repeated the little mime in quickened tempo and suddenly were laughing. Claude caught her in his arms, hardly knowing what was happening. In a minute, they were on the bed, and he made a tremulous discovery of her body naked. Although thirty-seven, he had never had sexual contact before, and the experience, if not very successful, was amazing to him. They were in bed for hours.

When Fritz Baird, an old cowboy, stopped by and discovered Mary, Claude knew Bart Fleming would soon find out about her. Bert was on a trip, but due back soon, and Claude worried. Bart might not like his having a girl — a squaw. Maybe he (Claude) should kick her out before Fleming kicked them both out. Stewing about it over the next few days, he got very upset and abused the girl and called her a dirty Indian.

Bart Fleming had worked for Claude's parents when he first came West. They had owned a small farm that required no extra help, but Henry Keefer had known Bart's dad. They had taken Bart in to help him. Soon there was trouble. Henry felt Bart didn't do enough work and was only interested in getting things for himself. Shortly, Fleming did buy the quarter and build the shack where Claude lived. Then his holdings grew rapidly.

Claude stayed at home. His mother told him he must look after them in their old age. Marriage was out of the question. Years went by. One day, his dad bought a new car, and that very day, scarcely knowing how to drive it, he killed himself and his wife at a railroad crossing.

Claude began spending his time in the saloon. There was no one at home to tell him what to do. Soon his fields were weed-grown and his taxes delinquent. Broken machinery went unrepaired; his cows began calving in January.

In the middle of a dry summer, Bart Fleming stopped by. Claude's place had a good well. Fleming had bought out a neighboring ranch and needed water. He offered to pay the back taxes plus a few thousand dollars for the place. Claude hesitated, but Fleming said he could live in the old shack for free. Help with the cows. Bart would let him sell a few head every year for spending money.

That was their arrangement. Claude bought a Buick, and soon most of his money was gone. Now and then, Bart singled out an old cow and scribbled off a bill of sale for her, and Claude took her to town. He helped with the branding and kept an eye on the cows on his part of the range. He was glad to be told what to do, but Fleming mystified him. Sometimes he came and talked to Claude in long monologues, complaining about his wife or worrying about money. "She whines that I don't give her nothing," he said, on more than one occasion. "Hell, what does she need? I don't have nothing. Leastwise, I don't spend no money on myself. Foolishly. Which is what she wants. Piddle it away. Women are the damnedest deal! You're lucky, living like you do. Sometimes wish I was back here."

Often he sat on the doorstep, talking on and on, apparently not expecting a response. Claude stood over him, leaning against the doorjamb, shifting now and then uncomfortably.

"Hell, you think I got a lot, huh, because I got some land and cows? Well, that ain't all there is to it. A man never knows where he is. Ain't never got it made. I come here as a young fellow thinking a herd of cows was the end of the rainbow. Lot of worry is what it is. Hell of a lot of taxes. And for what? The old lady still bellyaches day and night. Food's no better than it was when I was broke. I ate beans then. Hell, I like beans. Hardly ever get them any more. Yeah, you can count yourself lucky. Count yourself lucky!"

Other times, he bawled Claude out, reminding him of his position. "There's a critter with a horn growing into her head down there," he might complain. "Damn it, why do I have to look for things like that? I keep you around here to watch after the cows. You better remember that. You better toe the mark, by God! I'm letting you live here; I'm giving you cows to sell for your goddamned beer.

Where the hell would you be if I kicked you out, huh? You couldn't make it on that place you had. Your old man, he called me a good-for-nothing, the sonofabitch! Him and that dinky place he had. He was the good-for-nothing! And you! You're just like him. I'm the one that's made something of himself, and don't you ever forget it, Keefer."

When angry, Fleming paced up and down, never looking at Claude. He was a big man, red-headed but bald. Claude was afraid of him. Alone, in the safety of the shack, he raged: "Goddamn you, Fleming, we gave you a start. You had nothing! Nothing! You **were** nothing!" In front of Bart, however, he was meek. He ran when Bart commanded.

Worried then that Bart might not want him to have a woman, Claude yelled at Mary. But at night he was sorry. In the darkness of the bed, she was something more than a dirty Indian, and he tried to undo what fear had compelled.

Bart, when he finally came, was not angry. Mary seemed to awe him somehow. Claude caught him watching her furtively, but he did not speak to her. Claude hadn't specially noticed before, but Mary wore no underclothes, and her dress clung over her breasts and hips.

When Bart left, Claude was puzzled and uneasy. He studied Mary secretively and concluded there was something disgusting about having tits and a wide butt. Fleming was laughing to himself. **Keefer's got a** squaw! Yet Claude did not want to jeopardize the night; he went no further than warning Mary: "Watch yourself around him! Look out what you do and say — the way you stand around and the way you look. He owns hundreds of cows, you know."

Claude was careful to show Bart he was looking after things. He rode fence, reported a crippled cow, drove in a bull that had broken his penis. He went to town less frequently and drank less beer.

Through the winter, they lived together. Claude saw himself differently. He kept cleaner and dressed better. Yet he rarely took Mary with him in his car. She was a source of both pride and shame, and the growth of the former accented the latter. Because of her, he began to think of owning a ranch — yet a rancher shouldn't live with a squaw. Sometimes he brooded, sometimes he cursed Bart Fleming, and sometimes he quarreled with Mary. But largely he let the days go by, and nothing came to a head.

In the spring, they discovered that Mary was pregnant. Claude hadn't given that eventuality much thought. But the fact jolted him. He rushed Mary off to the nearest court house for a license, and soon they were married.

Bart, over the months, had visited less frequently than before Mary came. But if he had not poured out his troubles to Claude, neither had he bawled him out. They saw less of each other, and Bart was reserved and sometimes a bit testy. Now, when Bart found out they were married, he stared at Claude momentarily, then dropped his eyes. "Married her, huh?" he said, as if it were an occasion for regret if not mourning.

That was all. Claude worried. He should have asked Bart whether marrying the girl was all right. Now it was too late. He blamed Mary and grew fiercely angry with her, telling her Bart didn't seem to like their being married.

"Leave then," was all she said. "Leave. Go away."

Claude fell into a morose silence. Unmanned by Bart and Mary both. The idea of a place of his own had a new appeal. Times weren't bad. Farmers and ranchers drove new trucks and tractors. But there was no way to get money — unless Bart would loan it to him. The notion caught fire. For days he turned it every which way in his mind. Sometimes he was ecstatic: Bart would give him unlimited help! Other times reason said there was no chance.

But a firmness was shaping in Mary's belly. At branding time, he would have to approach Bart. It seemed a brilliant idea: Bart would be happy because of all the calves! Get to him when he's in a good mood.

It took four days to work Bart's herd, for Bart kept the crew small and they only did a hundred head a day. Each day they finished the roundup early, driving the cattle between the V-shaped wings of a corral and separating out the cows. On the opposite end of the corral was the branding chute, beside which they built a hot fire. Bart's truck parked there provided a safe place for the vaccine and castration equipment.

On the first day, Claude did not speak to Bart about money. He watched him carefully, but sometimes Bart was in a good mood, and other times he glowered. Claude waited another day and another. On the last day, they had, in addition to the branding, a cow to dehorn. Claude realized it would be a difficult job — her horns were too wide for the chute, and they would have to tie her down. Nervous anyway because time was forcing him to act, he grew even more disturbed envisioning a stuggle with the cow that would get Bart heated up.

Bart said they would leave the cow till last. Seeing what he believed to be his only opening, Claude seized the moment. "Mary's pregnant," he began. Coiling a rope, Bart froze. "She's going to have a kid!" said Claude.

Then Bart looked at him. The side of his face twitched slightly, and Claude felt a cold drench go down his body. But he had to keep on: "She wants me to get my own place. I was thinking if you could let me have a little money . . . I'd pay you back, understand!"

Bart looked at his hands, passing the coils of rope from one to the other.

"I—I—I wouldn't need much. I—I—I could borrow from the—I could—I'd still work . . ."

"Let's do the calves," Bart said quietly.

Bart did the branding, and Claude noticed that he thrust the glowing irons sharply against the ribs. Yellow smoke curling up, and the calves bawled. "Come on! Come on!" Bart snapped as Claude fumbled to get the castrating bands on and Fritz Baird scampered with the vaccine.

They ate lunch under the din of bawling calves. Yet Bart seemed to carve a bubble of silence around them. Claude's hands shook, and he dropped a bit of sandwich, and Bart noticed. Claude felt he had given himself away.

It was late afternoon when they got to the cow. Bart got a rope on her hind feet, and then Fritz roped her around the neck. They stretched her out and put one front leg in the loop to keep her from choking. Bart got a crosscut saw and some kerosene to keep flies off the horn stubs. Claude held her by the tail, and she spattered grass diarrhea over his boots.

Bart grabbed the upmost horn and began sawing. The cow gave a deep tremulous bellow. Her tongue went out into the dirt and dung of the corral. She tried to twist her head, and Bart was almost thrown off balance. He jerked the horn viciously and shouted: "Hold still, Goddamn you!"

When the horn came off, he spun it out of the corral. A tiny stream of blood spurted two yards into the air. It sprayed over Bart as the cow struggled; drops ran down his face. He tried to get the other horn in position. The cow got on her belly and looked at him. The ropes had loosened somewhat. "Step on that goddamned rope!" Bart told Claude. Claude jumped to obey. His weight controlled the cow. Bart got her turned over and began to saw on the other horn.

Again the cow gave a mournful bellow. She was not only hurt but mad. When the saw bit deeper, she wrenched herself, pitching Bart over her head so that he stumbled but didn't lose balance.

Coming back, he knelt and gripped the horn, puffing, enraged, pitting his strength.

Again the cow heaved. Bart slipped; quicker than sight, her horn entered his left socket and gouged the eyeball out on his cheek. Again he recovered himself, again with sheer will, he mastered the brute strength, sawing until the horn came off. For an instant he held it, presented it — to the cow, to the men? — and then, in a gesture contemptuous even of contempt, flung it out of the corral. Once again, the blood sprayed over him, but he ignored it, putting out his hand.

Claude didn't see what he wanted, and in a moment Bart snapped his fingers sharply. "Where's the kerosene? Get the lead out of your ass! What's the matter with you? That squaw got you petered out?"

Claude scrambled. As Bart took the can, his fingers brushed Claude, leaving a sensation like a burn. Bart dashed kerosene on the stubs, dropped the can and stepped close to Claude. His dangling eye was whitish, bluish, red-streaked, and drops of blood from the cow lined his face. "Listen, Keefer," he growled, too low for Baird to hear, "don't come to me asking money for your goddamn squaw! I bailed you out on that other place, and I gave you a roof over your head. Nothing was said about moving the Reservation onto my property then. You been selling my stock! Them bills of sale don't mean shit, because you never gave me nothing for the cows. Now I let you have a squaw, so don't start gimme, gimme, gimme. You get your ass back to work, or I'll have it in jail!" Then he turned and started for the truck, as if only at this moment the pain had caught up with him.

Fritz let the cow up. "I'll drive Bart to town!" he yelled. "He's got to see a doctor!"

As the truck pulled away, Claude went to his horse. Bart's face was imprinted like a sharp flash of light on his retinas, and he felt somehow accused of the injury. **Hundreds of cows; thousands of dollars — and he's mad!** Claude whimpered as he rode. The bills of sale no good! He couldn't move away — couldn't leave or he'd go to jail. **Oh, Jesus!** Again and again the lightning went through him: **He's got me, goddamn him!** He bellowed less in rage than in fear now even knuckling under wasn't possible. Bart had all those cows, while he (Claude) was married to a squaw. He raced toward Mary, his comfort; he railed against Mary, his curse. He wanted her before him to listen to his story and see what she had done to him.

Arriving home, he turned his horse loose and almost ran to the house. Mary had just finished a bath. She stood wrapped in an old housecoat brushing her hair. The washtub, half full of water, was in the middle of the floor.

She smiled as he came in, but the smile quickly faded.

"What are you doing taking a bath?" Claude howled. "You got me in trouble with him! The critter knocked his eye out, and he told me I don't own nothing. I don't own nothing and I could be put in jail! Them cows I sold. Them bills of sale! I can't go off and get me a place — I can't even leave if he don't want to let me. He's got me! He's got me! All because of **you!** Everything was all right till you came along. I've worked for him and worked, and now he calls me a squaw man. 'That goddamn squaw got you petered out?' That's what he says to me. Eyeball out on his cheek hanging there like a dead thing!" Claude's voice was shrill and rapid. "I ain't a squaw man; I ain't never lived like no goddamn Indian. It's you that's the Indian. I never would have asked him nothing if it hadn't been for you. Now he's mad, and he's lost an eye. I don't know what he's going to do. And you're the one. I never had no trouble before!"

Across the room from her, he sat wearily and looked at the floor, sighing like a scolded boy. It came over him anew how wronged he was. "I **married** you!" he complained, "but what have you ever done for me? Got me in trouble! I got no one to turn to! No one gives a goddamn about **me!** I've got nothing. I'm already getting old, and I got nothing!" He wiped his eyes and stared at the floor again.

The room was still. He became aware of himself blubbering and looked up slowly at Mary. She stood across the room like a statue, watching him, nothing in her face but a searching alertness. She seemed not so much **Mary** as simply **Indian**, quietly judging. A wave of hate went through him. He snapped to his feet. "**Are you smiling at me?**" He began in a low, savage whisper that exploded into a shout: "**Are you smiling at me?** You're the one that's to blame! You're the one, goddamn you, and you smile at me?"

She clutched the housecoat and drew back against the wall.

"You goddamn Indian! You goddamn **squaw!**" Head pulled down and shoulders high, he began stalking her.

Her mouth fell slightly open and she moved along the wall.

Stabbing suddenly with a finger, he screamed: "You think you can laugh at me? You're a goddamn **Indian!** You're a goddamn **squaw!**"

He moved round the tub one way; she circled the other, tensed to spring.

He made a start. She jerked away. He showed his teeth; made

another start. Again she jumped. She looked to the door, but he cut her off. A triumphant violence flooded him. He laughed without smiling, and his shoulders rippled with power. With a quick step, he got round the tub, and now she was cornered.

"Smile at me again! Go ahead, smile at me!"

She flung herself past him. He did not grab her, but stamped and shouted: "**Hah!**" Barefooted, she kicked the tub, splashing out soapy water. Then she limped to the wall.

Claude kicked the tub with his boot, for a moment sympathetic. But she turned defiant eyes on him. He felt an ambiguous need to catch her.

He began stalking again. "What's the matter? Scared of me? Don't be scared of **me**. Nobody's scared of **me**. I don't own nothing. I'm a squaw man. Why are you scared of me? Huh? What's the matter, can't you talk?"

She watched him, fire-eyed and silent.

"C'mere." He was sorry, and fearful of what he had done—yet ambivalent. He stalked her to catch her now; to hold her and overcome what he had made happen. She tensed visibly. He snatched the sleeve of the housecoat. Quick as a cat, she was free, springing across the room. Claude leapt after her. She rounded the tub and would be clear for the door and gone. His long grab caught a handful of flying hair just as her feet hit the spilled water. Slip and jerk together slammed her neck on the rim of the tub, and she rolled onto the floor quivering violently. After a moment, her body was still.

Claude stood beside her, arms dangling. "Hey! Hey, what's the matter? Hey, you all right? Come on, get up!" His voice grew sharp. "What you trying to do? Scare me? What the hell's the matter with you, goddamn it!" His mouth went dry and his voice broke to a whisper. "I was just kidding you a little. I didn't mean nothing." Trying to swallow, he choked. His whole body felt like a foot or arm that has gone to sleep. He felt apart from himself and heard himself mutter: "Hey" — and a recognition he had tried pathetically to conceal tricked him, mocked him — "you ain't dead, are you?" The light was fast being crowded from his eyes, and he dropped his head and hung on at the rim of consciousness. The light came back partially. Successive moments reduplicated the unmasking of reality. His sense of time was gone. But at one point, he was able to rise and get to the door. No one, nothing outside. Shooting the bolt, turning heavily, he found his strength gone, like a man in a dream who is pursued. His arms would not lift the body. Puffing, whining, he dragged it foot by foot into the bedroom and pushed and stuffed it under the bed. Panic tried to catapult him back to the tub, but his limbs refused and he lay down on the mattress. Again time was a black distance, and then he lumbered up from the bed with some strength. No one outside. He got hold of the tub and heaved it to the door. Mary had usually emptied it at the east corner, and now Claude did likewise and hung it up behind the house.

There was still water on the floor and a small spot of blood. Claude grabbed the first thing in sight — the dishcloth — and scrubbed hard. Tears flooded over his cheeks. "I didn't mean to do anything," he whimpered. "I **didn't** do anything. I didn't hurt her. It was all an accident. An accident."

Clambering up, he sped outside to check the tub. There was no blood visible on it. Nevertheless he wiped the rim several times. The sun was like a red bead on the horizon, and the evening was still and sweet. It seemed to him then that the whole thing could not have happened. Earth was calm and unaffected. Mary would come to under the bed and eventually laugh at him for putting her there. **I should have put her on** top **of the bed!**

Back inside, he pulled her out and began talking to her. "Come on now wake up! What's the matter, huh?" He baby-talked: "Oo going to seep aw day and aw night? Tum on. Tum on. Ain't oo going to get me thum thupper?"

He patted her cheek, and the head rolled, and his whole mood inverted instantly. He jammed the corpse under the bed, flung into the other room and opend the door. No one in sight. He went to the middle of the floor and got down, studying the place, wiping it with his shirt sleeve.

Weariness overtook him there; his body almost irresistably settled to the floor. His head ached. His mind reached for sleep, trying to shut everything out. But anxiety drilled his brain. And then there was a sound — tiny, unidentifiable, but it snapped him into a crouch. **Bart was at the door!** Claude froze. The figure outside was also frozen, waiting. But there was not just one; the place was surrounded. At any moment, they might crash the door. He listened. Time was undefined, except for the thumping abandon of his heart. Finally he stood up. A sense of self-possession in surrender filled him. He opened the door, ready to explain that it had been an accident. But there was no one there. Nothing: the safety of aloneness he had hoped to escape.

It was getting dark. Claude, his nerves still a shambles, nonetheless found a simple voice of reason intact. The dead woman must be buried. He was looking absently upon a cluster of miniature buttes two hundred yards from the house. The work of rapid erosion, they had steep sides and flat tops, like great tree stumps. One in particular was well shaped and as high as his ceiling.

When the sunset had faded, Claude got his spade and went to this little plateau. He made footholds and climbed to the top. It was largely covered with prairie cactuses — an area the size of his floor, canted slightly to the east. He selected a spot near the east edge and marked out the grave in his mind, head toward the sunrise. He was aware of himself as the only strange and frightening presence.

Once underway, his labor felt good. Its purpose became secondary. Work was penance; he felt better. The night darkened around him, and then the sky was richly salted with stars. Wholly engrossed, he measured himself with the spade, and chopped out the necessary length. He removed the cactuses with a spadeful of dirt so that they could be put back — a grave covered with them would not be dug up by animals. Such practical details flowed through his mind with comfortable detachment.

When the horizon lightened and the moon rose, he was almost finished. The grave was about two feet deep. He lay down in it to check the measurement. Rest felt good — but then the dirt seemed to close in upon him. He was dead, yet alive in death and helpless to protest the smothering of his body. Suffocation sprung him out, choking for air, and he slid down from the butte, sprinting off in an incidental direction. The shadows moved; cactus and sage tangled him. He spun round, flailing convulsively. But then he froze, shivering, and the world grew quiet again; fear became fear of discovery once more.

A purposive machine took over in him now. He scurried, half-crouching, to the house and dragged the body from under the bed, wrestling it onto his shoulder with no new emotion. Getting to the butte was easy, but climbing it proved another matter. His foot slipped half way up, and the body tumbled in a knot on the dead earth, which was barren here and brightly lit. He got it again on his shoulder and heaved himself up along the difficult footholds. At the top, with puffs like sobs, he lurched to the pit just in time to get the slipping body into place. Then he straightened it on its back and sat down on the bench at the foot end, oddly comfortable in the exhaustion of his sensibility. Her face was in shadow; the misshapen moon lit the rest. Her housecoat was wrapped around her waist.

His spirit was becalmed. Nothing existed save in the focus of his eyes; nothing moved in him but the habit of desire with a restorative promise in mad and tender fantasy. Scarcely aware of his physical movement, he sank down upon her.

With the bursting of his charged excitation burst his whole spell, and in that instant, fixed foremost in his mind was an impression of a stirring in her belly. He drew back with a hoarse cry and clawed himself up onto the mound of dirt. His stomach rent itself, expelling bitter fluid. The very atmosphere was sentient now, thick with accusation. This, like his rage before, was a trick to damn him. **A shadow! Bart!** Only an owl through the moon. But spurred by the flicker of light, the lance of terror, he snatched up the spade and whipped dirt into the pit as fast as his arms could jab. When it was full, panting, sweating, he tramped it down and then replaced the cactuses. Scarcely pausing to look again, he slid down from the butte and tore out the footholds.

Exhaustion caught up with him in the house. He fell on the bed in his clothes and was almost immediately asleep. But before dawn broke, terrible nightmares wracked him. He awoke springing upright and was unable to remember the cause of his misery. But then it came back, scorching through him like a cold fire. He felt she had come back and was under the bed to mock him. His head, when he stood, almost blinded him with pain. His balance was off, and his walk was drunken. Lighting the kerosene lamp, he got down. Nothing under the bed. But there was a spot on the floor that might be blood. He got the dishcloth and scrubbed. Then the spot stood out because it was wet and clean. So he got a pan of soapy water and lay on the floor under the bed rather than moving it, for that did not occur to him. He kept on until the floors in both rooms were finished. By that time, the dishcloth was black, but Claude did not notice and hung it on the stand where the dishes were washed. Hunger gnawed, but he hardly felt like eating.

The sun came up like a giant searchlight focused directly on him. The world was violently real. Every track, mark, disturbance was vivid, etched by the sun's brilliance. Bart would come any time to ask questions and spy around the place. **How come you washed the floor? What did you dump out here?** He had the uncanny feeling that Bart already knew. Bart would snoop around for a long time. **Left you huh? Left you?** He would keep asking about Mary. Finally he would say: **Let's go out and climb that little butte there, huh?** Bart would grunt a surly laugh the way he did when he gave Claude a cow or spoke of Claude's position with him. They would climb up the butte, and something — a badger perhaps — would have dug out a corner of the grave. That was as far as the vision went. Claude felt Bart's triumphant look, charging him with the damaged eye, smiling an open-ended threat.

In one way the fantasy was real; in another, he did not believe it and was struck by the idea that he could go away — now, and Bart would naturally think Mary had left with him. Without stopping to think it over, he got into his best clothes, locked up the house and headed for the city at a reckless speed in his old Buick. Just across the city limits, a policeman pulled him over. "Race track's the other side of town, buster." But instead of giving him a ticket, the officer ultimately said: "I'll let you go, mister. Ain't never seen no one take a warning quite so much to heart."

Claude crept on down town then. The lights and traffic kept him distraught, and there seemed to be police cars everywhere. At last he found a parking place and got out, feeling conspicuous. He rushed into a dime store to lose himself, but the clerks kept asking if they could help him. Finally sheltered in a men's room, he tried to think things over. **Go on — go to the coast!** This was as far as he had ever been, and he couldn't imagine working in an entirely different area. If only there were someone to tell him what to do! Bart was the only person he could think of. At last he went into a saloon and began drinking beer. After several bottles, his mind was freer in its perspectives. He focused on the idea that Mary had died accidentally. It was true in a sense that he had participated in the accident, but hurting her wasn't his intention. They had been playing, scuffling, laughing. She had dodged away and slipped. Who would know the difference — **who would care, since she was a squaw?** He experienced a rush of relief. No one would call him guilty.

But he had buried her. Why? they would ask. Why? **What a fool!** No one would have asked about a goddamned squaw. He sat brooding, drinking more. Then he said to himself: **Hell with it! Hell with them all!** No one was going to ask about a squaw. He'd say she left. Bart would accept that. But it struck him that Bart might miss him. He wanted to be home in case anyone came snooping around — it was important to know what they saw.

He rushed from the saloon and drove back the way he had come, speeding, swearing at patrol cars that did not materialize. His mouth was dry and his body soaking with sweat as he pulled into his yard. **Bart?** His eyes searched. No one was about. No fresh tracks of horse or car. He jumped out — and a bolt went through him: ragged black buzzards circled over the little butte, flapping, dropping from sight, rising.

Claude uttered a little cry and charged out to the butte, harried, baited by the images he invented. The buzzards were not landing on it, but some distance beyond. At that spot, Claude discovered a rabbit carcass, left perhaps by a hawk or owl.

He turned away, not relieved, but with renewed guilt and a sense of foreshadowing. He clawed his way up the butte to look at the grave. It seemed not so well disguised as he had imagined in the night. There was loose dirt around it, making an outline that looked shockingly like a grave. A little rain would wash this dirt into the grass. But his hopeful glance found no clouds in the sky — only a small airplane hanging in the distance. He crouched impulsively, although it was far away.

But what if the cactuses died in a six-foot-long yellow rectangle. It would be perfectly visible from the small planes that occasionally flew over. **Carry water! Wash down the dirt! Wet the cactuses and grass so they'll root again!**

He slid down and went and got a pail of water. Carrying it up entailed scratching and kicking new footholds, and all the time he kept looking around, expecting Bart to appear suddenly beside him. Finally the well — a poor one — was dry, and still the dirt showed, and the wet cactuses showed, and the little plane droned on the horizon, going the other way now. There was nothing to do but give his efforts over to the sun. He slid down and used the bucket to scrape away the footholds. Now that side of the butte was quite scarred. Maybe a few buckets of water would harden and heal the dirt. He splashed some on as soon as the well ran in. When it dried a bit, it looked exactly as if someone had gouged a strip up the side and then splashed water on it.

Claude went to the house and sat on the step, holding his face in his hands. A realization was slowly born in him: all the trips to the butte had made a dim trail. He started up. Never had he gone to the butte before last night, and there was no admissible reason for going. **Brush out the trail with a weed!** But then the brushing would show. **Brush the whole area!** He saw himself sweeping the front yard, while Bart, having ridden up behind the house, sat on his horse and watched.

Make more trails! He sprang into action, scurring back and forth, first out this way, then out that, always on the watch for Bart. When finished, he saw immediately that the effect was absurd. The trails went nowhere and had no excuse for being there. He sweated miserably for a while, and then a new idea struck him: **drive some cows through the yard!** Then there would be nothing but tracks. The cows never came around his buildings, but they easily might.

Claude wasted no time catching his horse in the pen out back and galloping to find some cows. It was too soon after branding for them to be easily rounded up. He ran them helter-skelter, with no conceivable reason to offer Bart if he came along. Soon Claude was weeping like a ten-year-old. But finally half a dozen cows and calves ran inadvertantly in the direction of his place, and he harried them along. Once they were in front of his house, it was not difficult to herd them back and forth. Shortly the ground was cut up with tracks.

Claude had a moment's respite and unsaddled his horse, even laughing a little although his feeling was not clear. Surveying the tracks on foot, however, he again despaired. They signified for him all his desperate antics, and surely Bart could read what was written in them. But at last he realized that there was nothing to do; that each further effort had made things worse.

On edge and unreal to himself, he hulked about, so fearful of Bart's coming that at last he began to long for it. Let it be over. An endless dialogue of questions and answers went on in his mind. Where is Mary? She got mad at me — took off. The cow tracks? He was trying to cut out one with a bad eye (there was always one with a bad eye). A spot of blood? He had shot a rabbit. All these things went through his mind in a serious rehearsal that quite engrossed him.

In the late afternoon, weary in body and spirit, he lay down on the bed. In his dozing, it seemed that Bart came, and they were in a corral with cattle. Bart was not angry, but he was dominant and full of the world. "I know," he said. "I know." And Claude got down on his knees in front of him saying: "I didn't mean it to happen. But I'll never expect anything again or ask for anything." He felt a sense of peace. But then Bart told him soothingly: "She was just a squaw." The words seemed actually spoken in the room and brought him awake with a start. Dozing had taken away his defenses, and the words felt viciously ironic. They ran through his mind: **she was only a squaw**; his guts knotted.

Soon it began to get dark. Bart would not come that day, and whereas before Claude had seen vengeance in his coming, he now read it in Bart's absence. Nothing was to be got over with. He had to wait through the night; maybe through the next day. Perhaps Bart was still in the hospital; perhaps the eye had become infected. **Oh, God, no!** That seemed the worst thing that could happen.

The darkness was oppressive. He tried to get supper, eat, wash up as he had done before Mary came, but it was all mechanical. When the dishes were done and the blackened dishrag wrung out and hung up, he broke into sobs — rending sobs that heaped him on the floor. Weak and ill, he stayed there, looking about the room. Every shadow was alive and had an attitude. Yet nothing would speak to him; nothing would give him the comfort of condemnation.

A scraping sound came to his ears. He could not position it or tell how loud it was. A burst of panic spun him one way and then the other. But now he spied a large beetle crawling across the floor. He caught it and put it outside.

Stretched on the bed to recover himself, he became aware of a spider dangling in the corner. There was a noise of wings past the roof. A cricket shrilled once and was silent.

Claude got his shotgun and loaded it. There was something outside the house — not Bart, not anyone. He blew out the lamp and stood very still, the gun across his belly. Silence — yet it was there. He did not know how much time passed. The presence grew less physically threatening. Claude unloaded the gun and put it away.

"All right," he said aloud, his voice husky and strange, "I'll turn her over to you. It was an accident. I buried her because I thought that was best all around. So go and do what you want to with me."

He went outside and got the spade. The moon was up. Incongruous with his present overt intention, he circled to the butte so as not to renew his trail. He chopped footholds and in a minute stood over the grave. The cactuses came out easily this time. He worked fast, but then, after several spadefuls, his thrust went deep and the blade struck something firm. A wave of nausea went over him, and reality shifted: the phantoms of his mind vanished into simple, literal facts. The body was here, concealed; no one knew; no one had to know.

Slowly then, he scraped the dirt back into the hole and replaced the cactuses. With a gut-level sense of finality this time, he turned away, descended and followed his circuitous route back to the house. Hopes of disclosure and confession were gone. He would bear the full burden of her death alone and suffer the imprisonment implicit in that freedom. He was stronger than the shadows — ever so little, yet stronger — and could not escape the fact.

Next day, Bart rode in.

He came early in the morning while Claude was making breakfast, and his knock at the door sent a drench over Claude. Bart thrust the door open after a few seconds. His appearance had changed considerably. A black patch covered his left eye and seemed to pinch his face toward that side. The other eye was bloodshot and avoided Claude's glances. "We got to get busy building that fence if we're going to have a hay crop. You only just having breakfast?"

He had spoken of the fence before — it would keep the cows out of a meadow so that the grass could be cut.

Claude scurried between the stove and the table but did not answer.

Bart moved restlessly up and down the room. After a few moments, he asked: "Where's the woman?"

Claude had been waiting for the question, yet it loosed a shock wave through him. He feared for his voice. "She left — run off." The words were a croak. He faced away from Bart, expecting more questions. Bart said nothing. Claude saw his hands shaking half an inch as he served his fried eggs from the skillet. One egg almost popped onto the table.

Bart said. "Left you, huh? Well, that's a woman for you!" He grunted a mirthless chuckle. "You'll learn about them. You'll learn! Don't let it get you all rattled." Claude sat at the table. Bart watched him for a moment, then slapped him on the shoulder with his gloves and said almost sympathetically: "Figure she took all your troubles along with her, huh? Well, I might as well go back and get things together. You come on up as fast as you can, huh?"

Claude nodded.

Bart hesitated. "You ain't still figuring on pulling out on me, are you?"

"Oh, no!" Claude spattered his mouthful of egg across the table. In the same instant that he saw a door of possibility open, he heard himself close it. He glanced furtively at Bart.

Bart lingered, meeting Claude's glance now, smiling somehow awkwardly. But he favored his blinded side: it did not change; only the right half of his face smiled.

For an equivocal second, Claude wanted to retract his words, but under that look he could not.

"See you up there," said Bart and left.

Through a window, Claude saw him mount his horse, then stare at the ground. But some explanation for the tracks seemed to offer itself in his mind, for he turned the horse and rode away.

Claude had been prepared for a resolution: either Bart would know, or he would not and the worry would be ended. But nothing had happened. Claude still had an uncanny sense that Bart knew or could find out. The prospect of being indefinitely in limbo made him bellow and crash his knife and fork against the wall. Bart's smile was imprinted on his brain — two things in the same face. He couldn't finish his breakfast.

He met Bart up at the Fleming ranch, and they drove out to the meadow. Claude's job was to sit in the pickup's box and drop steel posts everytime a large measuring wheel made a full turn. Then he and Bart walked back, driving the posts in with a heavy mall. Claude gave himself almost desperately to the work, feeling a comfort and security in it.

Claude ate with the Flemings at dinnertime. Bart's wife, who was always a bit peevish, waited on them. Claude kept his eyes on his plate, and at one point Bart remarked about his being down in the dumps. "His squaw's left him!" He grunted a little chuckle. His wife said nothing, but sent a disgusted look Claude's way.

Claude's nerves were taut, yet he saw that Bart interpreted his worry as sadness over being left. The idea of this misplaced sympathy in view of the truth rent him with emotion, choked him. He had to pretend his food had gone down the wrong way.

"God, man!" said Bart genially, "don't croak yourself over it!"

Claude expected to be bullied and threatened, but as they worked that afternoon, Bart kept his voice down and even made a few jokes. He seemed to be trying to cheer Claude up. Claude managed something that sounded like a laugh now and then.

So it was in the days that followed. They built fence and repaired fence, and the work was so tiring and so steady that Claude slept well and ate well and had little time to brood. Bart was friendlier than he had ever been before. A year ago, he had either bawled Claude out or complained about his own troubles; now he talked man to man.

One day he clapped a hand on Claude's shoulder as they walked to the pickup. "Well, we're sure getting a lot of work done, huh? Guess maybe you'd like a couple of critters to sell. I ran in two dry ones last night, old devils. You might as well drive them home with you and take them to town." That evening, Bart made him out a bill of sale, drawing the words slowly with a stub of pencil.

As he drove the animals home, Claude felt pleased, but resentful of his pleasure. He was quite sure now that Bart had no inkling of where Mary had gone. Why should he (Claude) be happy about two old cows? Yet the good feeling persisted in him for a while. Next day he took the cows to market in an old trailer, he spied a new calf with its mother along the road. On an impulse, and as a kind of revenge against the gratitude he hadn't wanted to feel, he stopped and caught the calf and put it in the trailer. It was not difficult to imitate Bart's scrawl and add "one calf" to the bill of sale. Bart had only marked one price for the two cows, and that would do for the calf as well.

At the sales ring, he suffered misgivings, and afterwards drank several bottles of beer. Back home, he brooded and was depressed and experienced some physical pain in his shoulders and loins. The shack seemed unbearable, silent and empty. From now on his life would be nothing but hard work and hollow nights. No wonder Bart was smiling and slapping him on the shoulder.

He looked out at the little butte. It caused no special feeling. He went out and climbed it. The grave did not show; the grass and cactuses had rooted. For a long time he stood trying to feel his earlier anguish, testing his emotions. Only a dull, ugly emptiness fill him.

A few days later it rained. A sudden, rapid downpour washed out all traces of his scratching on the side of the butte. Like an ablution, it cleansed his world. Thereafter, Claude watched Bart carefully and grew certain that he did not suspect what had happened to Mary and would never find out. Claude discovered that he could feel contempt for Bart. He watched his boss and saw that he was a slave to fences and cows like himself. For all his money and land and herds, Bart had to sweat and listen to his wife's belly-aching.

As the summer wore on, Claude grew adjusted to the reality of the stump butte. He had had to guard himself against surprise remembering with its stab of anguish for so many weeks that control became a habit and the butte gave him a kind of power. He **knew** and had survived, while Bart did not know. Claude was able to face Bart with a feeling that there was nothing Bart could do to hurt him now. He believed that he could survive even the disclosure of his secret.

But this sense of freedom had its price: without fear his life was dull. The long agony of coming to accept what had happened, the slow inner alchemy of grace, had been a profound experience. He was no longer the Claude of early spring. He had endured his life before, but now he was bored. Yet there was nothing else that interested him, and besides, he wanted to be around to watch the butte.

Next time Bart gave him a cow to sell, Claude also loaded up two yearlings and changed the bill of sale. Another time, he loaded up two unbranded calves and forged a bill of sale.

Not long after that, Bart rode in with a 30:06 rifle in a scabbard on his saddle. His face was flushed, and the tortured quality of the left side had taken over all of it. His eye did not look at Claude. "Couple of cows with tight bags out there. Somebody got the calves. Ain't seen any goddamned Indians around, have you?"

Claude said he hadn't.

"The sonsofbitches better not be. It'll be good-bye Indian if I catch them. Are you keeping a lookout?"

"Yeah! Yeah, I been riding regular."

"You damned well better be! That's what I got you here for. I'd bet anything that good-for-nothing squaw you had up here told her relatives. There's been rustling going on for quite a while. I been missing some critters."

After Bart left, Claude realized that he had got quite shaken up. For two days there was a knot in his belly, and he worked eagerly. The third day, he became angry and sullen. **My good-for-nothing squaw, huh**? he thought. **Indians, huh**?

On a day when Bart took his wife to the city, Claude loaded a calf and drove to the Reservation. He had met some Indians at the saloon. They didn't ask for a bill of sale. One of them had a sixteen-year-old daughter, and Claude had a hard time keeping his eyes off her. Finally he returned the price of the calf and got the girl in the backseat of his Buick.

Drunk on the experience, he raced home. For days she was on his mind, until at last he got another chance to see her by giving her father money. Bringing her home, near the little butte, was out of the question, but nothing kept him from visiting her on the Reservation. He was giddy with the idea of it. **Such a young one, too!**

One day, the Indian said: "Bart Fleming has a young black bull. I have a good friend called Black Bull. I want to give him that critter. We'll butcher it and have a good time. You bring me that critter, and you can have the girl anytime you want until she gets married."

Claude agreed. But once more by himself, he worried. Calves all looked alike, and Bart couldn't be sure of what happened to the odd one. However, the bull, a purebred Angus, was special. Bart might go around the Reservation asking questions. Claude sat on his step and brooded, gazing at the little butte, feeling sure that he had better not try to steal the little bull.

Days passed into weeks. He worked with Bart, and sometimes in the evenings, drove to the Reservation. The Indian made fun of him: "Where's my bull, huh? What's the matter? You think I tell Bart Fleming? I don't tell Bart Fleming."

Claude watched Bart carefully. Bart was no longer so quiet-spoken with him. Things had got more as they used to be, in previous years. Bart stayed on the lookout for rustlers and always carried his 30:06. Claude thought that maybe Bart suspected him. The idea of his guilt and the idea that Fleming was in the right felt ugly in him.

Fall and winter stretched boringly ahead.

Claude felt himself under tacit indictment — yet why should he be? He worked as hard as Bart. They rounded up a hundred steers to sell, and Bart shouted at him: "Come on, Keefer, get the lead out!" Bart now called him by his last name again. Sulking, calculating how many thousand dollars the steers would bring, Claude made up his mind. A sharp prickle went through his middle. He no longer felt gloomy.

A few days later, he parked the car and trailer near a corral in a little draw. Then he rode by the ranch. "Going to take a swing through the south pasture," he told Bart.

"Yeah. Good idea." Bart's eye searched him. The right side of his face was pinched now, as though the eye was pained from overuse.

Claude started out south, but over a hill, cut east. Bart's face hung before him. He was racked, vertiginous, driven. Whipping up his horse, he galloped the bull into the corral, slammed the trailer against the chute, harried the animal into it. Frantic now, panting, he dropped the endgate, bolted it, sprang around to the door of the Buick. There he froze for an instant to survey the rim of the high country that stretched westward to the ranch. In that instant, a 30:06 bullet tore away his brains.

A Country for Old Men

When I come out of the house after taking an extra minute to finish reading an item on seed wheat, he is sitting on the step. He has his town clothes on — a felt hat with only a few grease marks on it and new tan pants and a work shirt with the top button buttoned. A pregnant cat is rubbing against his leg. He is watching another cat, a scrawny creature in cat adolescence — from the previous litter. He has lots of cats and feeds them Purina Cat Chow and is now worrying because he's out. They'll get hungry while he's gone. Let them catch mice, I think; let them eat cake. But I know what's on his mind — he's mentioned it twice in the half hour I've been waiting for him to get dressed.

I'm taking him to the Fair in Aureole because he likes to look at the new farm machinery on display and maybe glance at the commercial booths and watch the pulling contests. Years and years ago he used horses. They gave him nothing but trouble I've been told. Then he got a tractor. It gave him nothing but trouble. His life has been nothing but trouble. He should have been a professor, not a farmer. I'm a professor. I should have been a farmer I sometimes think.

But not now; I don't think it now as I pause in the shade of the porch. He is on the step, sitting in the sun. The thermometer says ninety, but he has sat down in the sun. My reflexes halt me at the edge of that relentless brilliance. I dread even the memory of endless, thirsty hours in the fields watching thunderheads build in the west, knowing they won't ever reach far enough to cool me. But at eighty he sits in the sun. And I think, yes, this is a country for old men: it keeps some heat in their bones.

"Well, let's go!" I say — loudly, for he is almost deaf from all those days, months, years on the hammering tractors. We head for the car — my car, the spiffy new Audi. He likes the idea of it because it's German. He's German — first generation American; I'm second generation. But the German make doesn't mean a thing to me; I just like the car. Twenty years ago, he spoke of getting a De Soto. He wanted a De Soto when his big wheat crop came in. It didn't, and he bought a second-hand GMC pickup. It still runs, but he doesn't drive it on the highway; couldn't get his license renewed.

As we leave the yard, we pass the W-9, the tractor he's used most recently. But it's broken down and worn out. That's the problem now — our problem. That's primarily what's on my mind. We've got to talk about it, my brother and I. He's our uncle, and we've got to make a decision.

What do you do with an eighty-year-old man who can't hear, can hardly see, has lived about all his adult life alone, a bachelor, on this patch of indifferent ground; who constantly wrecks his machinery because, despite his unsparing efforts, he always overlooks one thing or another — to put the air cleaner back on or to drain the block before the first freeze. Yes, there are lots of things you can do: hire someone to help him or put him in a home or take him into your own home or just tell him to quit farming. There are lots of things you can do; just no right thing, no good thing. He wouldn't hold still for having someone else come on the place and do the farming; he'd die in a home; and it wouldn't be much better in someone else's home. Nothing for him to do. If you get him a new tractor — can he learn how to use it? How long will it be before he breaks the engine? What if something happens to him because of the new machine? How will you feel then?

We are at the gate and turn onto the graveled country road. It is August. The grain is cut. He turns his gaze over a neighbor's field. His memory is clear and his mind bright in many ways. His laugh has not really changed over the years, and he laughs now.

"They plowed up that quarter to plant wheat. The price went up and they thought they was going to strike it rich. Now the price is down and they didn't get a hell of a lot off it anyway."

I decided to try to get him talking. He'll entertain himself then, and I can either tune in or tune out and plan the day ahead. "Was that quarter ever homesteaded?"

"Huh?" he asks.

I try again, looking at him so he can see my lips and speaking a bit louder.

"Hell, yes!" he says. "Fellow name of Simmons. Before my time. Pete Olsen's old man tried to get hold of it then, but Myles got it away from him. Simmons broke half of it, but then it went back — damn near all back to buffalo grass. Now the kid — what's his name?"

"Byron," I say.

"Everett?"

"No, Everett's son. Byron."

"Yeah. I can't keep up with them."

Maybe they're something like his cats, I think.

"He broke it again. Hell, I'd've left it grass. Ever since I've been here somebody's been trying to get rich quick going into this or that. Ain't none of them got rich yet."

I look across the stubble — not really sparse; certainly not thick. What did it go? Twenty bushel? Thirty bushel? What is this business of gambling your life away for twenty bushel, thirty bushel? What is it that's **there** before my eyes? I went away, got educated, read philosophy. I can ask those questions: what lies behind the appearances? My body sweats. Only the motion of the car makes a breeze to cool me. Only the sunflowers are green — and yellow. They alone can look into the eye of the sun. Dust tunnels our wake; meadowlarks flitter casually across the road. Is there any depth to this fantastic, strange-familiar show? Who-what's behind it?

The old man is saying: "Yeah, everybody's gone crazy over wheat farming. You ought to talk to some of the old fellows around here."

I wonder who he means. I wonder how he sees himself. He's the oldest person I know. Maybe around seventy-five or so he got tired of thinking about being old and began to think in young terms again. Can a mind be old? I think of Merlin in **Camelot** — he doesn't grow old, he "youthens."

But now there is another field beside the car; another history. Somebody long dead homesteaded here. The old man starts telling about the tribulations connected with this piece of land. There's no house on it now. Maybe somewhere, in some corner, there's a hole that used to be a cave or root cellar, but I can't see it. And I've travelled enough now to be able to mingle the familiar and unfamiliar — where am I? Could this just as well be a piece of ground in Wyoming? In Spain? In Africa? I feel a touch of fright.

The old man is swearing vigorously. He's worked himself into a passion. Somebody paid two dollars an acre for the land once. The crooked politicians — Democrats in particular — are to blame for the inflation. I hear the names of Hoover and Roosevelt, but I am thinking about a medium-sized star on the edge of an average-sized galaxy. Ten billion galaxies within reach of Palomar telescope. Teilhard de Chardin said all that vastness makes us not insignificant but extra special. But that doesn't solve the problem of what to do about the old man.

My nephew, ten, will take him to the fair. Good. I can get away to do his grocery shopping then. A big sack of Purina Cat Chow. Grapefruit. Canned ham — he likes ham. Eggs. Coffee. Damned Safeway bread. Aren't a lot of the additives in ham and bread supposed to do you in? But he's eaten them regularly and he's eighty. Who knows? One day he may be ninety. Okay for groceries. What are we going to do about the tractor? It's shot. It needs a complete overhaul, but it might as well be junked. And already he should be working the summer fallow one more time and getting ready to cut the cane. Then there'll be the winter wheat to think about. Sure, we can ask the neighbor to sneak in and do part of that. He'd be glad to. But that only defers the real decision. Are we going to buy him a new tractor? His money, of course; no problem there. No, the problem is a bit nebulous and easily sentimentalized, but it is very much there. Old lady Olsen, Pete's wife, said: "Why does he have to go on working?" Exactly the kind of incisive analysis of the situation we need.

I take him to my brother's house just outside Aureole. Mother lives next door. My brother manages three places in addition to working with our uncle. This keeps him busy approximately twenty-four hours a day — but as he says: "I like a bind." He wouldn't know what to do if he weren't hassled. I come back part of each summer. Soon now I'll have to head off for the coast again to get my classes together. Then I'll be concerned with how to engineer the division of English 451 because you really can't teach all of twentieth-century American fiction in one class. And then there'll be the question of whether Tweedledee or Tweedledum should chair the freshman English committee. How did I get into this business?

At this point, I can't really remember.

The old man takes his box — with his banking paraphernalia and seed bills — into the house. The boy, my nephew, is ready to go. There's nothing he'd rather do than take the old man to the fair and look at the tractors with him. They'll spend hours looking at the tractors. They'll have icecream cones. The old man will try to show the boy this or that, but he'll get it mixed up, and the boy'll end up showing him. They'll sit in the shade a while. Then they'll go look at the livestock. Then they'll go back to the tractors. The boy has said: "If he gets too old to drive a new tractor, I could drive it."

"You're too young yet," his dad told him.

"I'm ten. How much older does a person have to get?"

I look at the old man; I look in the mirror. I wonder the same thing.

We all go down to the fair grounds. I pay the admission, and then I worry a little bit out loud whether they'll be all right. The boy reassures me. The old man'll take care of him and he'll take care of the old man. I know he's right, and so I leave them. I head down town, hoping I can find some shade to park the car in. I could have got air conditioning, but there's something sissy about it. Does it make sense to drive in an air-conditioned car to a field in which you're going to sit for ten hours on a tractor in the scorching sun? No. We weren't "put here" to be comfortable. Comfort (I think, as I walk with relief into the air-conditioned store) is part of the American syndrome. The so-called conservatives sell it to us for their personal enrichment; the so-called liberals universalize it for political power. But people get the politicians they deserve just the same as they get the gods they deserve — it's all part of the same thing. One day they'll be wiser. Feeling wiser already, I get a shopping cart and head for the pet-food section.

Later on, in the afternoon, I go back to the fair grounds and look for January and May. They are sitting on a bench in the shade of a tree. They do not see me right away. They both look tiny. They are in similar positions: knees apart, hands gripping them lightly. But I note a difference in their eyes. The boy is looking at something outside; the old man is looking at something inside. His eyes are unfocused. Where is he? Has he gone backward in time? Is he here, at this fair grounds forty years ago? Is there a woman in the picture? Is he thinking of some road not taken? Or has he simply tuned out completely? Is he in some other dimension? Has he abandoned this hunched, static body to enter an unimaginable region? I have a sudden sense of utter triviality of death. It is a thing for the young to brood on — but the old have no time for it —it is already part of their past.

"Did you look at the tractors?" I ask.

"Yaa!" cries the boy, his face and tone insisting on the significance of it all. "I showed him how to run all of them."

I assume they did not actually start any of the engines but went through the motions.

The old man has not yet noticed my presence.

"Well, good!" I say, gazing at the lot where the tractors are parked — most of them huge machines with cabs, air-conditioned no doubt, and fitted out with CB radios. They cost as much as a two-bedroom house in Aureole. More in some cases.

But the boy makes a conservative ploy — if you don't ask for too much you may get it. His voice changes to quiet and serious reasoning; he points to a smaller machine, but one that nonetheless has a cab and more power than any machine the old man has ever owned. "All we really need is one like that. I can reach the pedals if I scooch forward on the seat. If he couldn't drive it, you know, I could drive it."

"You'll get plenty of tractor driving when you get older," I say, knowing the boy won't be able to imagine what farming really means, the hours of your life you have to trade for a field of wheat. He is not thinking at all of the hail storms that may rob you of your tractor payments or of the so-called free market that allows Wall Street to manipulate your product to keep you poor while people prosper who have never spent an hour on a tractor and are contemptuous of the very thought of doing so. The boy doesn't understand that, nor does the old man who year after year at the polls accepts the same old cliches of a free market and less government.

Still, you can't operate without equipment. I don't want to disappoint the boy completely and say: "We'll see. I suspect you'll get to drive a tractor in a few years in any case." I walk around so that the old man can see me. He is not startled, but lifts his head and allows his eyes to come into focus slowly. He takes me for granted.

"Ready to go?" he asks.

I nod. "Have a good time?"

"Huh?"

"Did you have a good time?"

He gives a little laugh. It maybe wasn't the thing to ask. It calls his attention to himself, and he isn't really sure how good a time he

has had — his life has not been lived for good times. "Oh," he says
— and his undecided mind shifts to something objective and specific — "they sure think they need big tractors nowadays. Ain't hardly
a farm around here needs something like that."

I smile and nod. He and the boy get up and we head for the
car. I push my hat back and wipe the sweat from my forehead.
My eyes flirt westward over the hills hoping to see a thunderhead.
There is none.

II

The old man's life has not been lived for good times. It has been
lived for work. His god is not the fruit of labor but labor itself. In
the past sixty years he has gone to church only for funerals. Yet
he is a kind of monk; a protestant monk standing in direct relationship to his god and ever at his devotions. His matins have been
curses at tractors that won't start in the morning and his vespers
curses at seeders and cultivators broken in the day's operation.

His father was a German immigrant to Wisconsin, a kind of
refugee from Bismarck's armies who worked in an iron foundry.
Very young then, this now-old man went to work for a rural neighbor. He arose at four to milk six cows before breakfast, spent the
day in the fields, and after supper milked the six cows again, cleaned
the barn, fed the pigs, chickens, guineas, horses and fell into bed
at eight to rise again at four and confront the passive, ruminating
beasts whose udders refilled themselves interminably.

He ruptured himself trying to lift a rock that had to be removed
from a field. Thus he did not have to go to the Great War. Instead
he went West. Once again, he traded his labor (wearing a truss
over his hernia) for a place to sleep and something to eat and a dollar a day in the summer. Hearing of some land for sale, he went
to look at it, driving out with a rented team and wagon. He felt
the soil and asked about water. There was no well, but he walked
into the middle of a forty and stood with his hands on his hips in the
sun riding glorious and benevolent and eternal in his own free sky,
and he said yes. He bought the forty and rented another hundred
and twenty that belonged to the same quarter and dug a cave and
built a shack and went to work on a well.

He had a neighbor witch the well. He saw the forked branch turn
down as though the Earth Spirit herself had reached up with an
invisible hand to point her secret treasure and promise her silent
beneficence. Borrowing a pick and a shovel from the same neighbor,
the young (now old) man went to work by himself. He meant to get
help when the hole became too deep to throw dirt out of. But then

his inventive mind devised a machine by which he could trip a bucket of dirt into a chute and work all by himself. He took great satisfaction in being able thus to continue working alone. He had a keen sense of specific operations but little sense of overall management. When twilight came that day and he decided to quit, he realized that the structure supporting the pulley wouldn't support him. There was no way out of the hole he had dug. He spent a cold night on the now sandy bottom of the well. Next morning, his neighbor looked down at him. The neighbor did not realize he had spent the night there but told him he might need another rope and secured one to a post and dropped it down.

Perhaps the young man should have taken his experience as an omen — sold the land and journeyed onward to the distant Pacific shores, as, later, one of his wayward nephews would. But maybe also something in him already knew that it made little difference where the plodding drama should unfold. Here as well as there he could heave his rock to the mountaintop and see it roll back and call himself happy.

He hired a local ne'er-do-well to haul up the bucket, and at sixty feet he was standing in water. He installed a steel barrel with the top and bottom cut out for a reservoir, finished plastering up the sides with cement and chicken wire, built a platform, set up a pump.

How must he have felt that first evening when the hired man left and he was alone with his creation? The eternal chariot reddened on the diurnal crest and then, on sudden cue, all the stars sang out together. He had no thought of a medium-sized sun in an average galaxy — here, on this middle isthmus of Being, was set the center of the universe and it offered him world enough and time. Yes, now the very way of things would shape, as from his own body, the figure of a woman, and there would soon be the avian consonance of child voices in the cool shadow of the new, the big house that they would build. He could go back to Wisconsin and all his bearing and the car, the woman, the children would say: I have done it, I have made it.

He brought home first, as he had to, not a wife but a cow, timeless gynandrous symbol of the primal union — and she drank the well dry. Day after day the narrow castiron sluice, thrusting horizontally from the pump in ambivalent erection, sputtered its seminal insufficiency for his thirsty vision. The rod of the diviner had not lied — except in spirit, in the Earth Spirit, in the great she-side of all that is. For the betrayal touched every dream.

So he dug another well, simply guessing where he might strike water. This well was dry.

So he acquired a team of horses, a plow, a disc, a harrow, a hand broadcaster. He planted and the grasshoppers reaped, and he sowed for a harvest of hail. Ephemeral rainbows arched cruelly in the wreckage of his wheat. Yet he salvaged a bit of corn, sold a few pigs, worked and finally moved to another piece of land. There he dug more indifferent wells; watered two cows instead of one.

His younger brother came out to help him. The brother got land of his own. He married and had children.

Their uncle dug another well, and this time he struck an aquifer that wouldn't run dry. He built beside it the house in which he would live for the major continuous part of his life. Now he was ready.

He courted for a while the sister of his sister-in-law. But somehow, in her presence, his house, his well, his fields did not seem enough to offer. He waited for an unequivocal indication that she wanted him and would be satisfied. Then an earlier beau came back one day with a green Chevrolet and rose-colored daydreams, and she ran away to marry him.

The not-quite-as-young man bought a tractor, a Farmall Regular with lugged iron wheels, and sold his horses. He spread hopper poison, cursed the clouds, and set out to design the future's revelation.

But lo, when the next seal was broken, the sun became black, for dust mounted the hot winds and the beast of the marketplace cried: "A measure of wheat for a penny, and three measures of barley for a penny." The crops grew pale and brown and shrank into the powdered earth. Only Russian thistles thrived. They grew huge as washtubs and dried and rolled with the shifting winds, shelling their seed into every inch of the ground until their spidered skeletons were caught in the web of barbed wire. Then they gathered the drifting dust. Like snow it filled road ditches and buried four-foot high fences. A not-so-young man went to bed and an old man got up to meet his red-rimmed eyes in the mirror and feel his belly hollow and his mind amazed.

Every day the sightless scorch of the sun looked down; every day the hustling winds razed the fields. Every day the young-old man worked, worked. He built a hen house; built a hog house. Maybe chickens and pigs would yield a profit.

The seasons turned. He borrowed money for seed and money for fuel. He saw his tractor slowly wear out; fatigue entered his bones as a permanent condition. It became the physical coefficient of every gesture. Work was what he had, was all he had, and he heard its Gloria Patri in the yammer of worn connecting rods.

"Life begins at forty!" cracked his brother. But for him there was neither beginning nor end now. There was only the long, long row that spiraled into eternity.

III

Supper over, the old man is stretched out on the sofa napping. He is totally bald, and the circle of his crown is white where his hat has kept the sun off. His face and the back of his neck are brown from constant exposure, but the crown is white in startling contrast. His lips are full from his false teeth; his closed eyes are circled hugely with a dullish purple like washed grape stains. He is probably not asleep, but no matter — he can't hear us anyway.

We are at the table yet, my brother and I. Mother and my sister-in-law work at the sink. The little boy and his sister have disappeared.

"Well, do you think he liked the fair?" my brother asks.

"He seemed to. They went through the tractors with a fine-toothed comb."

He huffs a chuckle. "What did he say?"

I know what he means now. He doesn't mean only what did he say about the fair. He means did he say anything that might help us. Did he say I don't want a new tractor; I'm ready to retire. I tell him we didn't raise the question at all, feeling a little guilty that I haven't somehow made an attempt to solve the problem.

We are both silent then, looking at the table.

"He could get him a trailer house up here," Mother ventures. "Have a garden. He sits in the house and reads a lot of the time down there now. Why couldn't he do that up here?"

Why couldn't he? Because there's another dimension. She knows that really, but I try to think how to say it to her.

Then my brother, drawing some abstract of his conception on the table with an index finger, tells a little story he hadn't told me before. "It occurred to me," he says, "that he might like to travel around the country a little. He used to talk about it. We could get a high school grad — some kid that wanted to see the country before he settled down — and pay his way just to look after the old guy. He's got a little money now. He don't need to work. I asked him about it. Buy a camper, I said; get a college kid to drive it. Go to Florida; go to California. Even go to Mexico."

He pauses. I wait.

"Well, he said he'd think about it. So he thought about it. Next time I saw him he said: 'I've decided what I really want to do is stay here and work until I die.' "

That's the other dimension. My eyes flirt to the sofa. I feel a little uneasy about the idea of discussing a person's future without his participation. I remember something Margaret Mead said. The way a society treats its old people is an index to its health. Something like that. The old man has been put upon by charlatans in recent years — fellows trying to take advantage of him; sell him one thing and another at an exorbitant price. That's the other side; that side of our society isn't so healthy. But right now we face a moment of truth as it were.

"What's he going to do?" Mother asks. "His tractor's shot isn't it?"

I nod.

"If you get him another one, he'll soon have it wrecked."

"Worse," my brother ventures, "he could kill himself. Suppose he gets a new tractor and puts it in road gear out on the highway and rolls it?"

For the rest of our lives we'd feel responsible.

"Have someone in to do the farming," Mother says. "He's got to face facts eventually it looks to me like."

"I suggested that to him," my brother says. "He blew up. He couldn't take that — having the neighbors farming his land."

"Well what are you going to do then?" Mother asks — someone has to precipitate a decision.

I review in my mind certain possibilities we haven't mentioned. I could give up my job and come back and look after the old guy. Giving up my job might mean in effect giving up my career, since academic positions are almost impossible to find these days. What are the terms and/or limits of responsibility? I haven't been particularly close to or distant from the old man. In the old days, I might have farmed an adjacent section and helped him as a matter of course. Today I live half a continent away. What are the mores of this fluid society? How **does** it treat its old people?

My brother has in effect done all he can. He has practically managed the old man's place for the past ten or fifteen years, and that is why the old man has what money he has. He had not been able to rise out of debt since the Depression until his nephew helped him. But there are limits to what one person can do for another and still meet the terms of his own contract with existence. Just what those terms are is never wholly clear. We are negotiating the terms at this very moment. We are, in a qualified but very real sense, negotiating both the terms of the old man's death and the terms of our own future societal postures. Yet fate and the old man hold most of the cards.

We are silent for maybe two or three minutes. The superficial part of my mind goes off on a curious reverie: I wonder whether the old man has ever made love to a woman. Eighty years of life and not once, not one single time. Can it be? I conclude that it not only can be but probably is. Once he said: "If I'd got married I probably wouldn't have got so far." How does he see himself? I muse that the dignity of man derives from something in him deeper than the pettiness that afflicts his daily existence. Why are there existences rather than nothing at all? Heidegger asked. That puts men and stars in perspective!

But to approach the problem at hand philosophically is to approach it wrong-end-to. My brother has more immediate, practical — and finally more appropriate — matters on his mind. We look up at each other together, spontaneously, and I have some sense of the general character of what he is going to say.

"There's a fellow lives next to the Fox-Creek place," he gestures vaguely, "who's got a 706. That's slightly bigger than a W-9 — six cylinder job. Eight speeds. In pretty good shape. He wants to sell it. Fifty-seven hundred. That's not bad. Not too different from what he's been running. Think he can handle it?"

I lift my shoulders. "How complicated is the hydraulic apparatus?"

"About like what we've got on the W-9."

So I nod. The decision has made itself as it must, and now we have to actualize it. The old man's health is reasonably good — if it fails, then the situation will change. But as of now, we are going to let him live the life he himself would choose, whatever the hazards. That seems the obvious, civilized decision — but it will continue to seem so only as long at it works out. If it doesn't work out . . . how do you look the old lady Olsen in the eye?

When he wakes up (for eventually he does go to sleep) we put it to him: there's this tractor — fifty-seven hundred dollars. He sits on the sofa, knees wide to support his forearms as he leans into the discussion staring through the carpet ten feet out. At first, I think he will be happy — a new tractor! But of course it isn't a **new** tractor — which would be only that much more different from what he's used to — and it strikes me that he's a little peeved after looking around at the fair. He'd like to be the one to go off and pick out a tractor. Something big and brand new that he and the boy could select together. He'd like to toss a check for ten or fifteen thousand on the desk and drive off in road gear. But reality does have its perimeters, and he knows it does.

He asks a couple of questions about the tractor's suitability for his machinery, and when my brother reassures him, he sits for a few minutes in silence and then says: "Well, yeah, okay."

"You take him down in the morning," my brother says. "I'll go with the truck and bring the tractor. Probably be down there around noon. I'll explain to you what you have to know about it, and then you can stay there with him and show him, because I'll have to get going. Keep out of the way of the wheels when he's on it. We'll hook it up to the rod weeder, because that's what he'll have to be using on that winter wheat ground. Get them little weeds so they don't take the moisture."

IV

So that's what we do. I take the old man home, and he feeds his cats, a sudden tangle of snarling appetites at his feet.

I suppose there are things we could do while we wait for the tractor. But the old man has his mail — including a couple of farm journals — and so we read. It is cool in the house, and it is getting hot outside. We have already had lunch by the time my brother arrives.

When we unload the tractor, the old man and the boy are beside themselves, although the old man is still trying to appear indifferent because he didn't get to pick the tractor. I spend most of my time keeping them out of the way. We don't want a disaster before we even get started.

"I know how to run it!" the boy tells the old man.

The old man laughs with pleasure and affection. My brother and I glance at each other and smile. The boy is too young to run the machine, but we realize that in a couple of years he will be old enough to do a little work anyway. The old man likes him and so there's no problem with that kind of arrangement. But it's nip and tuck. Can the boy grow up fast enough to take over from the old man? We can only wait and see.

We fill the tank with gas and hook up the rod weeder. It is afternoon by this time, and my brother is long overdue to supervise a second cutting of alfalfa on his east place, but he stays to run the machine and to make sure it's working right, and to figure out which gear to drive it in. I ride with him, and we decide on fourth. I take over for part of a round. It seems simple enough — if only the old man will listen to what we say and not try to go in fifth, which is first again in high range and may confuse him completely.

The old man and the boy stand side by side like two prairie dogs on a mound watching our every move.

When we finish the round, my brother has to leave. He takes the boy with him over loud protest. Now I am alone with the old man, and the tension of my responsibility is giving me a headache. I am ready to start explaining the operation of the transmission, but the old man is suddenly not interested. At first I'm confused, but then I realize that there's a certain indignity in his having to have me tell him how to run a tractor. He has owned tractors for fifty years and I've hardly clocked fifty hours all told.

So he finds something wrong with the rod weeder. He's been look-ing at it — I have to give him credit. The drive chain has a link that's about to break. How the situation could happen I don't know —maybe the old man ran a crescent wrench through it the last time he used it. Anyway, we have to take the chain off, remove the link and replace it. This eats up a good part of the afternoon, because the old man doesn't have a spare link and we have to go find one on a wrecked drill out back of the hay yard. It takes us a good hour to get the drill apart — and then the link doesn't quite match, but we use it anyway. I conclude that it'll work.

When we finally have the rod weeder in shape, the old man feels he has salvaged his dignity and is ready to hear about the tractor. Hoping I haven't forgotten anything, I get him up on it and point out the key and the starter (he has spent most of his life with crank tractors, although his W-9 was fitted with a starter). But, mainly, I show him the transmission. You have to put it in neutral to start it, and then you have to make sure you've got the right gear and the right range. "Be careful not to grind the gears," I say. But I know he can't hear the gears and will probably grind them every time he starts up.

You have to choke the thing to start it, but it can flood, and nat-urally it floods when he tries to start it. "You have to let it set a while!" I say. Now I feel he may think we've foisted off on him a tractor that isn't any good, but I know he doesn't have high expectations where machinery is concerned — he's been around too long.

After a while, I try it and it starts. I get him in the seat and sit on the fender, hanging on, and tell him to go ahead. He's excited, but he doesn't want to show it. He wants to be indifferent, and so, with a kind of shrug in his manner, he grinds the gears sharply, lets in the clutch with a jerk, and we're off. We make a round on the little patch in front of the house. As far as I can see, he's doing all right. I don't want to make too much fuss, but I ask him if there's anything he doesn't understand.

Of course he says there isn't. One problem he's noticed though is that the vibration of the engine causes the throttle to close part way. He thinks maybe we could hook a spring onto it to hold it open. We look for a spring and rig it up, and he exhibits an air of achievement. We grease the weeder, and I check everything I can think of on the tractor.

After that, he thinks he'll get something to eat and then start on the summer fallow in the west eighty. He'll work until dark.

I have supper with him, and he plays the radio and afterward lies down to have a nap. I begin to think he won't want to go out at all any more this day, but when the shadows are getting long, he suddenly arouses himself and is ready to head for the field.

The tractor starts all right, and so I wave good-bye and watch him go, hoping he doesn't take out a gatepost on the way. I walk back to the Audi and am ready to start home. Then I think maybe I'd better just drive around by the field and have a look to see if he's doing all right. I wait a while though. Let him make a round. I go in the house and look at **Newsweek**, and when I hear the tractor coming, I drive out to the corner of the field.

I walk onto the broken ground to see how well the weeder is doing. It is outfitted with a rod that is supposed to turn in the soil, pulling the little weeds under and leaving the field flat and clean. With satisfaction I see that the field is flat and clean.

The evening around me is sweet and still, except for the sound of the tractor, which alone moves, huge and powerful. The whole landscape belongs to the old man; he dominates it. Yeats said that Ireland was no country for old men, but I think to myself that South Dakota **is** their country. It makes young men old, but to the old it gives place and quietude — here if anywhere is the threshold of eternity. And the old man knows that he belongs here. I find that enviable; he has made the land his, and here he will plant his final seed, his winter wheat.

I expect the old man to stop as he comes around, but apparently he doesn't even see me. He is completely engrossed as he turns the corner. He has successfully completed a round, the farmer's unit for measuring field work. So he stands up now as he drives, a captain at the helm of a new ship he has taken full possession of.

"Ahoy there, Sisyphus!" I shout, but of course he can no more hear than see.

I watch for a while, and a diving nighthawk plucks a taut string in the breast of evening, and the old man darkens against a hill and emerges on its crest. From this angle I can't tell where the distal turn should come. He seems to be steering for the sunset. Its empyreal fire ignites the efflux of dust from his wheels: he is caught in a gyre of light.

The Jimson Chronicle

from

The Fullness of Earth

Bick Jimson came West in the early days of cattle ranching. He grew modestly prosperous. But then the homesteaders arrived. Unable to act in the face of radical change, Bick lost almost everything. But he left a small holding to his daughter Etta. She never married, but, certain she must realize love through the land, she spent her life building back the ranch. At last, facing death, she reached a final understanding; in a triumphant gesture, she willed the whole ranch to a young man who had come to work for her.

Bick Jimson: Rancher

Bick Jimson came out of a green New England with visions of red deserts in his head. Not up on his geography, he thought the West was all Arizona from the Mississippi on. But when he discovered brown prairies, Black Hills and white Badlands, he took these to be the true colors of cow country, and so he stayed in Dakota. It was 1877. The Black Hills had been opened to the gold rush. But Bick wanted nothing to do with mines. His was a cowboy's dream. He believed in an eternal West, vaster than the horizons of a man's imagination, where everything was possible: the terrible pleasure of danger, and the pleasant terror of boundless opportunity. He had faith that in the lawless, unmarked and unmeasured country, his design would prevail. The West, wild, vicious, open, was conceived in the female principle, and Bick Jimson would take her endlessly and in infinitely varied ways. Under the cathedral silence of starred, unreachable heavens, his spirit need recognize no limits — and because it was a bit devilish, would stand in favor with God.

The young Bick Jimson faced into life as one faces into a spring breeze. He was clever enough on the one hand to be able to dream on the other without doing his ambitions injury. He got along well with men, knowing intuitively that the majority of them are easy to get along with if you make them think you understand less than they do and occasionally need their advice. Self-respect one must keep, but it needn't engender a burdensome pride.

Bick got off a river boat at Ft. Pierre and soon found a group of men who intended to ride west to join the round-up with the Z Bell outfit. "I'd kind of like to ride along," he ventured, after listening to their talk for a while. When several of them laughed, he tried to look hurt — and in some measure was. But he hung around the saloon. They ignored him, and time went by. One man gave him occasional glances, and then finally caught Bick's eye and gave his head a little jerk. This man, graying, fortyish, introduced himself as Leighton and told Bick he could ride along if the trip wouldn't be too much for him. Bick thought it shouldn't and asked what a person had to take along. Leighton told him in great detail — even went along to a dry goods store and helped him pick things out.

But that evening in a camp by the river, Bick got the feeling that his initiation hadn't yet been accomplished. Somehow he was still alone. He expected some kind of a challenge — offered probably by one person. If there was a fight, Bick would wrestle, for he had learned to subdue his peers with a scissors hold across the belly.

Before long, a heavy-set, red-faced man with a rifle grew loud drawing everyone's attention. "I'm loading up my Winchester!" he roared. "Every critter this side the river better clear off." He leered this way and that.

"Oh-oh!" someone exclaimed, "Cook's got his gun! Stand in front of him if you don't want to get shot."

"Don't get behind him!" someone else cried. There was laughter all around.

"I can shoot the eye out of a jack rabbit at fifty paces!" said

Cook. "On the run!"

"You or the jack on the run?" Laughter again.

"You'll be on the run if you don't look out!" Cook leered. He marched through the camp and hung a tobacco sack on a tree trunk.

Men shifted back. "Clear a path! Broad as it is long!"

Bick laughed with the men, but he sensed mischief. This must have been a ritual that was performed before; maybe this time it had to do with him. He was excited and alert.

"Now," said Cook, returning to the group, "you are about to witness the slaying of that there tobacco sack." Then he spoke in a rapid chant: "Gonna stand right here with my face in a frown and my pants pulled up and my hat pulled down — and **shoot!**" With the last word, he threw the rifle to his shoulder and fired.

A splinter burst from the side of the tree six inches off the sack.

Men laughed and jeered. Cook pointed an accusing finger at the tree. "**It moved!** I saw it; it moved!" He strode up and down, taking high, clownish steps, enjoying himself in a display of mock vexation. Then he stopped with his back to the tree. "**This time:** gonna stand right here with my face turned away so the tree can't see when I'm ready to say . . . **shoot!**" Bending double, he threw the rifle between his legs and fired — missing the tree completely.

Jeers and guffaws sounded. "Wow!" "What a deadeye!" "It's even safe behind him!"

Cook strode up and down appearing to be genuinely angry. Bick wasn't sure whether or not he was putting it on. "You laughing at me?" Cook challenged the men. "All right, put your money up! Put your money up! Ten dollars says I can outshoot any one of you. Come on!" He thrust the finger toward Leighton. "Come on!" — inviting another man.

Then his eyes fell on Bick Jimson. "You're smiling, huh, young fellow? You think maybe you can outshoot me? Well, get up here and let's see it." Cook backed off, rolling his head oddly but keeping his eyes on Bick. "Come on! Put your money where your smile is."

Bick glanced around the group, sure now that the whole performance had had him in mind, but unsure that a simple contest was all Cook wanted.

A fellow who hadn't spoken to Bick before leaned close and said confidentially: "He couldn't hit the broad side of a barn from inside it! Shoot with him. You'll make yourself some money."

There was a moment of heavy silence. The men spat tobacco

juice or rolled cigarettes, but their eyes shifted to watch Bick. Slowly then, he got to his feet.

"Get your money out," said Cook. "Get your money out!"

"Two dollars," Bick told him. "I ain't got much."

"Two?" Cook exclaimed.

"Two against ten, Cooky!" a flat voice from somewhere taunted him. "Two against ten, deadshot!"

Cook hesitated — then growled: "All right. Two against ten."

Bick guessed that the men sitting about weren't on one side or the other at the moment. How they would feel about him depended on his performance. He had used guns, but never a Winchester before.

This time, Cook sat down as he prepared to shoot, aiming across his knees. Bick had learned to listen to inner promptings, and so he did not simply await his turn. He walked back and forth directly behind Cook, studying the rifle and the way Cook aimed it. Bick noticed that the rear sight was off center.

Crack! and the bullet struck the lower right-hand corner of the target. Springing to his feet, swelling like a rooster, Cook handed Bick the rifle. Since no rules had been established, Bick lay down, resting the gun across a fallen branch. Around him, the men were exclaiming humorously over Cook's success. Bick's eye centered above the barrel, and he guessed that Cook must have aimed with one corner of the sight rather than its notch. This also suggested aiming slightly low, since the corner was higher than the point of the notch. He pulled the trigger, but it went hard, and his eyes squeezed shut. So he started over again, taking his aim consciously and keeping it through the squeeze. This time the explosion surprised him; the kick against his shoulder caught his attention momentarily.

Immediately, and with scarcely a glance at the tree, Cook shouted: "**Ho! ho!** He missed! Missed the tree a mile!"

Before Bick could collect himself, a dispute was under way. "He missed." "No, he hit damn near the same spot." "Yeah, he hit; by God, he hit!" "Hit? You go to hell!" Several men scrambled to the tree. "He hit all right! He hit. There's two bullets went in there!" "Yeah, and the kid's is a nick closer to the middle!"

Bick gathered up the money — and then went to look at the tree. Cook was there, inspecting it, studying it. He looked not only bewildered but mad, as if he had been hit in the forehead with a stick. Rolling his eyes, puckering his mouth, he finally ventured: "Ain't clear. We'll do it over again. We'll try that one more time!"

Bick shook his head. A yankee trader doesn't repeat a deal in which he's come out ahead. "I don't want to take all your money."

"You already have!" laughed another voice.

"Two'll get you twenty this time!" cried Cook "Get down there. You shoot first."

"You ain't got twenty bucks!" the outside voice exclaimed.

"Two'll get you a saddle."

Bick shook his head.

"Got lucky and now you're going to quit, huh?" Cook grabbed hold of him and tried to push him down. Bick struggled, got an arm around Cook's neck — they fell together, and when they landed, Bick already had got his scissors hold, locking his ankles and straightening his legs with Cook's midsection in between.

"A-ah! A-ah!" howled Cook. "You're busting my gut, you're busting my gut! Let go! Let go!"

Bick released him and rolled away. Cook scrambled to his feet with groans and gasps. "I think I'm ruptured! Oogh; o-o-oogh!" All at once he began to undo his trousers and run for a nearby bush yelping: "Oh, Jesus! Oh, Jesus! Oh, Jesus!" with each jump. Some of the other men laughed.

When Cook was out of sight, Bick walked through the group. A few acknowledged him with their eyes; others looked reservedly at the ground. But he sensed acceptance; he felt his performance had Won the West.

And that was just as it should have been: the great, golden gate of his imagination opened, and he rode out the next morning into all the hazards of the new country like a child going off to feed uncaged bears in a park. Throughout the summer that followed, he survived everything: broncs, cows and country — and the further jokes and challenges of his fellow men.

Bick found that he could use the ideas people had about tenderfeet for his own entertainment. He had a taste for whiskey and allowed himself to be "introduced" to the cowboy's drink numerous times. Each time he rewarded his gloating benefactor with at least a small cough and choke. That usually ensured a second round.

Visiting Deadwood for the first time, he discovered that beyond all other charitable urges that take hold of men stood the compulsion to introduce a greenhorn to a brothel. Even the desires that attracted men to the brothels could be deferred for this gratification. Bick hadn't tried women, but he was sure they would compare favorably with whiskey. He let his innocence be known among different ones. Drooling and gabbling, they rushed him off to a parlour house — and he emerged to reward them with staring eyes and a jerk to his step. Several little groups ushered him off for a taste of honey — until at last, rushing about to tell the story, they saw what Bick had done.

Nothing more was said about it. Some of them acted a bit uneasy when Bick came around — and he smiled to himself and bought his own shot of whiskey.

He had an occasional turn at gambling also. But the game stirred no fever in his blood. He stayed in only if luck ran his way — thus over a period of time, he came out ahead.

All these little matters contributed to Bick's sense that the world was his oyster. The West was his journey into sin, beyond the strictures of his New England past; hence it was the proving ground of his genius. Working for the Z Bell, and later trailing in Oregon cattle, he learned all aspects of the ranching business. He learned that one didn't steal from his fellow cowboys or ranchers — only from the government and the Indians. He learned that the road to wealth is open to those who perceive and take their opportunities to travel it.

After a few years, Bick was ready to make his modest rise to fortune. The opportunity he saw and took came with the delivery of a herd of Oregon cattle — both steers and heifers — to the Pine Ridge Reservation. Some of the animals were penned. Others were left free, and the Agent let the Indians run them like bison. Bick watched. It was soon evident to him that the Indians had no sense of economy. They were interested in sport first, then food. Snow had begun to fall, and under its thin veil, Bick joined the hunt, harrying the strays down coulees toward the Nebraska border. Amidst the ridges and hills, galloped the Sioux, yelping and shooting; from behind every outcrop rose Bick Jimson, grinning and watching his chances. Once Bick got on the tail of a steer and then discovered an Indian also in pursuit. The brave kept firing at the animal and missing. Finally, Bick, who carried a Winchester on his saddle, took a shot at the Indian, for he considered the critter his. He missed, but the man fled. Afterward, Bick cherished the idea of actually having shot at an Indian and rather wished the bullet had connected. In his tales, his aim was better.

The winter that year proved to be one of the worst on record. But the storm in which Bick gathered cows was early and not very cold. He spent a bleak night in some junipers and rounded up with the first gray of dawn, heading south. A rancher on the Niobrara took him in. Bick traded a few steers for pasture and the rest for more heifers. He wintered on the ranch, exchanging his labor for board and room. His first calf crop was very late, but it increased his herd. The second spring, he moved north into Dakota just before the land below the Cheyenne was taken from the Indians.

Established in the midst of an open range with a modest herd,

Bick began to think about marriage. He was lonely. And now surely in the foothills of greatness, he saw no natural limit to his possible empire. But he ought to get married. So far in life, he had known coarse, sexual, apparently carefree women — and liked them. But marriage was a different matter. It had solemnity, a dignity . . . like death. He remembered his mother and the standards of a New England upbringing. After driving his cattle east to market one year, he spent some time in Mitchell, where he met a shy, conventional young woman named Elizabeth Fenner. He went back to visit her, and later they were married.

For a time the sudden imposition of structure and responsibility on his life was elevating. Sex as an idealistic experience rather than a physical revel appealed to the dreamer in him. He believed in the rightness of the marriage and in its spirituality. The young Elizabeth had a frail beauty that touched his heart whenever he looked at her. Building up the place and increasing the herd kept him home. He dug a well, put up hay, rode after his cows. But Elizabeth, used to "the East," was lonely. When she was seven months into a pregnancy, Bick sent her "home" to await the baby with her family. She was gone four months. During that time, Bick was in Aureole a lot and visited the saloons. He was almost thirty-five now, and while the ranch was growing satisfactorily, something gnawed at him. With Elizabeth gone, his heart reached backward for the old time. There was a freedom and excitement that was no longer within reach — but the fact that he yearned for it made Bick worry about his marriage. Not actively unfaithful to Elizabeth, he still longed for the physical, animal sexuality of his earlier years. Marriage and ranch confined his dreams — he was married to the ranch. Its development was fixed and predictable. He perceived a dilemma: dreams were unsatisfactory until they were realized, and once realized they were limited and measurable and therefore unsatisfactory. The horizons of the West and the horizons of man drew in. But Time was the Judas — Bick Jimson should have been forever twenty-one. From the fright of alarms distant yet within, he turned his imagination Eastward — not toward New England, but St. Louis and New York. Now the ranch, which he still wanted and must keep, became a means to explore a societal world of infinite possibilities.

This new vision was only an embryo when Elizabeth returned. Bick was not conscious of it as an intention; was scarcely conscious of it at all. He was amazed and pleased by his little daughter. Elizabeth was happier, less lonely. Bick dwelt upon the building of the ranch.

Yet each fall he drove cattle east to market and used the opportunity to travel on to Omaha, Chicago or St. Louis. On these trips, he met prosperous ranchers — discovered himself as a prosperous rancher. He enjoyed the nightlife of the cities, drank a good deal, spent a lot of money, and then went home to pretend to Elizabeth and himself that nothing had happened; that he was just Bick Jimson, rancher. He still leaned into life with a bit of a smile at the corners of his mouth. But a touch of flush was coming into his face. His belly sagged over his belt. His hair was going gray. And he was accompanied by a nagging presence, like trying to remember a missed appointment, unable to focus on what it was.

At the turn of the century, Bick decided to build Elizabeth a new house. The year before, she had suffered bronchial pneumonia, and she remained frail. The same year, Bick had gone as far as New Orleans on his trip after selling the cattle. He had not been intimate with Elizabeth, because of her illness, and in the French Quarter visited certain women introduced to him by a wealthy friend. Upon his return, he undertook the construction of the house. It was two years in the building and was never completely furnished. For Elizabeth once more contracted pneumonia, and this time she died.

Bick was hurt by her death beyond the residue of despair and loss he felt. It seemed a result of his interest turning away from her. The house seemed a cover-up; her death, his reality exposed. Although this feeling stayed with him, he did not face it squarely. In another part of him, there was a sense of release. The old, expansive westward-looking vision with its female mysteries of sin, now securely transmuted into an eastward-looking vision with societal female mysteries of sin, need no longer be held in check. His spirit was prepared to believe that the Judas Time might itself be betrayed. And so he dared not allow too much reflection.

As for his little daughter, he loved her. She was now almost eleven and rode with the men and roped and helped with the branding. She was old enough to take care of herself, and there was an old cowboy named Red Arnsdorf to keep an eye on her. Bick didn't worry — until he realized that for no reason, a female's reason, she wanted him home, or wanted to be with him. So he took her along. But that was no solution. Any trip with her became **her** trip, and he became fumblingly conscious of an absurdity in the revels his imagination had planned. A compromise then: he would spend some time with her on the ranch; some away by himself. After working through the summer months at home, Bick left with the cattle drive.

From Chamberlain, he went on east to Chicago, and from there to New York. Away and with friends, he didn't think of Etta so much and was gone for six weeks. He drank every day and enjoyed many women and spent over a thousand dollars. But at last there was nowhere to go except home.

Etta's eyes made him pay the price of the trip again. He understood that a young person's feelings are authentic; they mean what they mean. A sense of Elizabeth's presence accused him. The Dakota horizons grew ominous. He wanted to be away to escape the knowledge that his place was here.

As Bick prepared one day to ride to Aureole — a short trip — Etta came out to the corral in a white dress. Usually she wore pants and a shirt. Bick liked her to wear dresses. Her eyes glistened with tears, and Bick busied himself with the latigo, trying not to see. Then she said: "I don't care if you stay home or go away, Daddy. But I just like to be with you."

Bick felt a sudden pain in his throat. "I'll bring you a horse!" he told her, making a smile. " I'll bring you an Arabian mare!"

She tried to smile too, but he knew that gifts don't work.

And so, riding the long trail to Aureole, he resolved to get married again. This time, she must be the right kind of woman, sensual, strong — then he could settle down to what was his in the West and be satisfied. This was no easy decision; it frightened him. Inescapably his life would flow into hardened, predestined channels. But, he said to himself, the girl needs a mother. Perhaps it was through the moral that Time could be defeated.

Over a period of months, the idea of remarrying grew in its appeal. He even had in mind a particular woman in St. Louis — relative of a ranching friend. She was in his eyes a lady, and — if she were still available — she might set a good example for Etta.

When he told Etta his thoughts, she said: "You don't have to."

"Of course!" Bick told her. "You've got to grow up to be a lady. You've got to have an example."

She shook her head. "I'm all right," she said timidly. "You don't have to."

He believed she protested what she took to be his deference to her, and that reinforced his sense of magnanimity in the decision. She was shy, but he would do right by her!

Off he went that summer. Carrie Littleton, the woman he had in mind, was still single. Bick spoke to his friend, who, a day later, took him in a motor car — his first ride in one — to the great, three-story family home. Bick experienced the apprehensive excitement he had felt when being taken to the best parlour houses — Carrie, soft-bodied, humorous, talkative, evoked the gaiety and sensuality of women and places Bick had enjoyed most in his life. Yet she had a refinement and restraint which marked her as a lady in his eyes. She was gracious in her Edwardian gown and choker pearls, melding into the decor of an elegant room. It was spacious, yet full; a dark carpet reflected the floral regality of the walls, whose moldings echoed the high mantel and the sweep of the banister — recalling to Bick fine hotels and bars. There was rich, cushioned furniture, mirrors, a table with baluster legs, a walnut secretary, a chandelier. Huge oil paintings hung on the walls — one a portrait of a stockman, the other a scene of railroad building, filled with husky men and the steam and smoke of a locomotive, like an iron god, fierce and colossal. Between them stood Bick, adolescent and old, surprised to find himself so readily accepted where he was not asked to pay.

During the first few days of his visit, he became quite erotically stimulated by Carrie. Thinking of marriage and worried about his age, he purchased a Heidelberg Electric Belt. "The suspensory carries the soothing current direct to the sensitive sexual organism, saturating these nerves and cells with the vitalizing current. Every disorder and disease peculiar to these organs yields immediately. Also has stomach attachment for indigestion, constipation and general debility of the stomach." Buying Carrie the best meals St. Louis offered, Bick found immediate use for the stomach attachment.

He courted in style. Not asked to pay, he spared no expense, acquiring a 1904 Oldsmobile. This was a three-horse-power machine which let them ride conspicuously through the streets. In fact, Bick felt so conspicuous that he rarely kept his eyes on the street, but continuously looked about for people who were looking at him. One day he ran into the back end of a wagon, tilting a keg of spikes onto the engine. It was heavy enough to break down the front end, bending the wheels in, so that the car seemed to be ducking and covering its nose. Bick and Carrie had a crowd of spectators in no time — laughing girls and galoots pawing over each other to see. The wagoner began to shout and pound the car, until Bick told him he could have it if he would shut up and clear away the mess. Then the man began to dance and kiss the girls trapped in the inner circle, while Bick made his escape with Carrie.

Once out of the crowd, Bick became crestfallen at the realization that he had given away his Oldsmobile.

Carrie rolled her eyes, saying: "Well . . . I like closed cars anyway. Don't you? What could you do with that one out on a ranch?"

"I should have got some money out of it," Bick grumbled.

She slipped her arm through his. "Money don't make the world go round. Love does that! I bet you could buy a dozen Oldsmobiles and that big ranch of yours wouldn't even know the difference!"

Bick looked at her, and his sense of extravagance quickly returned. "It ain't the money. But I think it was the other guy's fault. He was driving awful close in front of me." In a minute he asked her how she thought she'd like living on a ranch.

She answered that some of her very best friends were ranchers.

"We're more than friends, ain't we?" he ventured.

She agreed that they were, and Bick seemed to feel a nudge from the Heidelberg Belt. Next thing he knew, a proposal and acceptance had happened quite painlessly. The car had served its purpose after all.

He returned to the ranch for the fall round-up. Etta went along on the drive to Chamberlain, and Bick was happier than he had yet been in recent years. Etta was growing out of childhood and into companionship. Bick had his vision of how it would be when Carrie came (although he did not speak to Etta about her very often). He would have on the ranch what he loved from both the East and the West. Carrie would warm and fill the house. Etta would grow more and more involved in the business, and she was opening new horizons in her own life, which he vicariously shared, and which represented a different kind of defeat for Time.

When he saw the bridge being built over the Missouri, he thought, well, yes, there'll be settlers for a little way. But not in the Badlands; not in the table country — that's only good for cows. He had known the West long and intimately. One glance should tell anyone it could never be settled or fenced.

Later that year he went to St. Louis and brought Carrie home with him. They rode the Chicago and Northwestern up from Nebraska to Aureole. Then Bick drove to the ranch in a buggy. As the journey lengthened and the road dwindled to a wagon trail, Carrie smiled less frequently.

"Great country, huh?" Bick ventured. "You'll like it. You feel close to God out here." It was the first time in years that he had used the term "God" without its being part of an oath.

She gave him a reserved smile.

Bick had grown used to his house and had stopped seeing it. When Carrie saw it, he looked with her eyes. It was a parody of the house in which she had stayed the previous summer. There were no carpets, no paintings, no chandeliers, no fireplace, and it had not been completely furnished.

Carrie's mouth had difficulty with its smile. She said, too quietly:

"Oh-h-h my-y-y! A real ranch house! An upstairs and porches even. I hadn't realized . . ."

Bick cleared his throat. "Hasn't been furnished — the furnishing. Better that way. You can order whatever you want from Sears. Damned good stuff from Sears, you know."

She walked slowly around the front room. Bick saw dust on the windowsills and chairbacks. It had probably been there since Elizabeth fell ill, but he had never seen it before. Carrie's eyes seemed to miss nothing, and there was no awe or excitement in them. An ambience about her condemned him as a fraud. He was a shabby little rancher who had represented himself in exaggerated terms. And Carrie was a woman he didn't really know. Her eyes finally came around to him, and only with an effort could he meet them.

They were interrupted by a clatter of sudden footsteps over the back porch. Bick turned to confront the apparition of a kind of Western Huckleberry Finn with girl's hair. Her boots and pants were covered with manure, and there was a streak of mud down one cheek. She froze at the sight of Carrie.

The silence hung there one moment too long. Then Bick straightened formally. "Carrie, I'd like to present my daughter. This is Loretta. Etta, this is Carrie, your new . . . uh, my wife."

Carrie said: How do you do, Etta?"

Etta dropped her eyes with a slight nod. Then, suddenly animated, she sprang toward Bick. "Dad, old Blizzard's down in the barn! He's sick! He's got the bellyache or something. Red's been working to get some salts down him. We tried to get him up. That's how I got shit all over . . ." She rolled her eyes toward Carrie, and her voice dropped to a mumble: "That's how I got dirty."

"Well, you go on back out there," said Bick. "I can't come right now . . ."

"But he might die, Dad! Red thinks he's going to die."

"Well, horses die, don't they? I've just brought Carrie home. I can't go off to the barn right away."

Etta's eyes strayed in Carrie's direction and came back to the floor in front of Bick. She caught a quick breath and held it. Then there was a new explosion of words: "Red's having trouble getting the salts down him. He can't hold him, and neither can I. We got to have some help. Red says he's going to die if he don't get that down him."

Bick scowled at her and then shot a smile at Carrie. "Well, all right, I'll come along for a minute." He excused himself and followed Etta to the barn.

The old white horse was on his feet. "You get the salts down him?"

Bick asked Red Arnsdorf.

"Oh, hell yes," said the old cowboy. "No trouble."

Bick looked at Etta. She hung back and kept her eyes down.

"Well, I'll go on in then," said Bick.

He started toward the house, Etta following along. When they were out of Arnsdorf's hearing, she burst out: "Red shoed Chief!" That was her horse. "I think he put too heavy shoes on him. They ain't for a saddle horse. Come and look at him. Can't run as fast as before. He don't like them."

"I thought we came out to pour salts down Blizzard," said Bick.

"But Chief's going to go lame! Come see. Them shoes are too heavy!"

Bick grunted and strode on. She grabbed his arm. Then he turned to her sharply and caught her by the shoulders. "Now, you listen to me! What's the matter with you? Coming into the house like that? Is that the way to have Carrie see you for the first time? Go clean yourself up and put on a dress. Carrie's your new mother. You want to make her proud of you. You don't want to run around looking like you're not even a girl! You've got to learn to fix yourself up the way she does." He smiled then and cupped her cheek with his palm. "Come on in now and get cleaned up."

Etta stood absolutely still for a moment. When her voice came, it was very tight. "I'm going to water Chief."

Bick went on to the house. From the porch steps, he heard the sound of galloping. Etta rode away over the stark autumn pasture. She did not come in until after dark, and she went to her room without a word.

In the meantime, Carrie had wondered out loud if they oughtn't to have a house in Aureole. Wasn't it a good idea to have a place to stay in town?

Bick thought about it for only a few minutes. Then he said that was probably a good idea. He realized that Carrie meant to live in Aureole. His life would be formally divided; things would not be better for Etta, but worse. Yet it took him only a few minutes to accept the crude irony and relinquish his vision of the way things ought to be. Instead of believing he must triumph, he thought in effect: **I will salvage something.**

And so Carrie lived in Aureole, and Etta lived on the ranch, and Bick spent some time here, some time there — and quite a bit of time in the saloons. Carrie did not complain about his being gone. But with Etta it was a wholly different matter. Sometimes she accompanied him for a few miles, when he rode toward Aureole, but other days she disappeared hours before he left. He saw her doing desperate things to please him — even cleaning the house. She tried to find problems that would keep him home. When he was gone and came back, one time she would meet him washed and smiling, in a white dress; the next she would be in dirty pants, with her hair like a rat's nest.

In a year the Milwaukee Road came through, and Pinnacle was founded. In the following two years, Bick Jimson's open range became a maze of barbed wire. Bick had a title to two sections. He might have bought more, but had not. He looked with stunned, unfocused eyes upon what was happening. And then he turned his back, facing into a bar, behind which, more than likely, hung a pastoral painting of a nude girl, and probably not far from it another picture called "Ten Thousand on the Hoof."

He talked with old-timers in the Custer Hotel. He was an old-timer, made so over night by the swift influx of honyockers. He was Bick Jimson: rancher — red-faced, mustached, wearing a ten-gallon hat, fifty-dollar boots, a silver-studded belt, a silk shirt, a bandanna. Holding a glass of whiskey in his hand. **Bick Jimson**. A young man, really. He had just four more years to live.

Etta Jimson

Loretta Jimson had abandoned her bedroom during a very cold winter twelve years before and still slept in her clothes on the velour couch her dad had bought from Sears, Roebuck for $8.75 in 1903. This morning, as every other morning, she awakened and lay for a while open-eyed amid her dusty furniture. A set of high-backed Irish dining-room chairs had belonged to her mother, but the other pieces were all Sears, Roebuck's: an oak table strewn with magazines and papers, a rocker, a love seat stocked with old copies of **The Cattleman**, a desk stuffed with fifty years' accumulation of bills of sale and cancelled checks — hundreds of thousands of dollars on paper, nothing ever thrown away — and in a favored place, a book of Golden Stamps she got for buying gas.

In one corner a floor furnace raged, filling the room with intense heat. Etta roasted self-indulgently under her blanket. But at last she squirmed and threw it off, starting up vigorously. **Can't waste time laying around! Have to get going!** In fact, she had stopped being comfortable, and her efforts took her no farther than the sitting position. Her shirt was wadded about her, and she worked it back and forth, scratching herself, tucking in corners here and there, while at the same time stretching her eyes wide open and then wrinkling her whole face to squeeze them shut. Her pulse came to her head in spaced bursts with the imperfect labor of her heart. It alone marked time. The clock had gone haywire a year before, and she hadn't bought another. They'd give her a mantel clock with enough Golden Stamps, and she'd have enough in another year. Elbows on knees, she braced her head against her pulse. Sleep had left a vague ache in her body that made her think of dry rot and gave an oppressive sense of death. But she kicked on her slippers and then yawned, working her fingers through her hair. Naturally curly, it had once been auburn, but was now a dull pinkish-gray, short and thin.

A sigh like a pleasant groan escaped at the end of her yawn. She knuckled her eyes and refocused them on the arch opposite her. There was a double crescent of hammer marks just at eye level, still exactly the same as the day they were made, when her dad had been finishing the archway, and she had tipped a sawhorse over, causing him to hit his thumb.

A few minutes later in the kitchen, she made her breakfast. She had put in a gas stove and electric lights when the power line came through, but largely she saw conveniences as inconvenient. She was sure plumbing would cause her no end of trouble. While she maintained a strict view of keeping the house neat and ordered, in fact she didn't want to be bothered with it and had grown oblivious to its dust and disarray.

A coffee pot jiggled on one burner; over another a skillet heated. Etta hewed pieces of bacon from a side and dropped them into the skillet — then carried a little piece of rind into the front room. There was a mouse-trap in the archway, and although it was set, the trigger had been licked clean of bait. She fixed the bacon onto the trigger and went back into the kitchen.

Her breakfast consisted of coffee, bacon and a few slices of store bread from a loaf on the table. She took no milk or sugar with her coffee. Her mother had always said: "Don't eat sugar. It isn't good for your teeth." Etta still had her own teeth — never brushed them, but never ate sugar.

She chewed luxuriously on the thick slices of bacon. When her dad was alive, they had had steak for breakfast — steak all the time, except when her mother fried a chicken defiantly. Then her dad felt obliged to look sour, but he didn't say anything, because secretly he liked it. All her life Etta had thought about getting some chickens but had never done it. Most of her meals consisted of bread and Dinty Moore beef stew from the can. She bought it by the case, and in one corner of the kitchen a pasteboard box was piled high with empty tins.

Etta mopped her plate with a last bite of bread and stuffed it in her mouth. Then she splashed a bit of scalding coffee onto the plate and rubbed it with an old flour sack. Back in the front room, she sat down to pull on her boots. A movement in the archway caught her eye. There was a mouse at the trap, and Etta drew herself up, holding her breath, watching with annoyed fascination. The trap was hard to spring, and every time she baited it, the bacon was soon gone. But she did not try to set it fine; instead, she waited for the mouse to get too smart for his own good. Then . . . **BINGO!** That would be the end of him.

In a fever of tiny activity, the mouse stretched to nip and hunched to chew, stretched and hunched, until the bacon was all gone. Then it began leaping and tumbling around the trap in a kind of dance. The old woman got angry. She picked up a boot, but decided it would be lethal and drew off a sock, wadding it and hurling it. Like a flash the mouse was gone under a door. But instantly it reappeared, sniffing up and down the sock, nose quivering with interest.

"Well, for . . ." Etta got up. The mouse fled. The old woman limped across on her one high heel, snatching up the sock to pass it by her nose. "Limburger for sure!" She threw it toward a door, beyond which was a porch where she did her washing. From a chair back she got a clean pair, put one on and dropped the other across the couch where she would find it that night when she had the other boot off again.

Now she got into her winter coat, tied a scarf over her ears and pulled on her hat. On the back porch, she tore three pages from a Sears catalogue — Sears' paper was best; she had even quit buying from Ward's — and headed for the barn. A hired man had fallen through the outhouse floor last summer, and she hadn't got it fixed yet. Walking told her her hemorrhoids were giving trouble again. When she had had her heart checked, the doctor had told her about some suppositories, and she had bought some while filling her heart prescription. But she had left them too close to the furnace — then kept forgetting to buy more.

Thinking of the suppositories reminded her that she had forgotten to take a pill this morning. **It's another pain in the ass.**

Anyway, the hemorrhoids weren't bad enough to keep her bowel movement from being a great satisfaction to her, and afterwards she burst from the barn with considerable energy. **Now to get at it!** But she stopped after a few steps, as she stopped every morning, because she was never able to remember the terribly important job she had meant to "get at." She stood frowning, hunched against the wind. Visions of the big jobs went through her mind — haying, branding, shifting the herd. It was none of those matters today. Then, triumphantly, she hit upon it: **Take that pill. That's what I was going to do!**

Back to the house she went and took the pill. On the way out again, she carried a hammer and spikes. **Got to fix that chute before I can brand!** At the corral fence she rested, catching her breath; then she went on around it, through a barbed-wire fence, picking up a plank on the way. The corral was old. Its poles were badly weathered, the posts that held them rotten and sunken, and here and there, pieces of woven wire or sticks filled holes haphazardly. The whole structure leaned precariously against its own curvature, encircling half a century of trodden dung. But Etta saw only **the corral,** and passed on to fix the chute. She pounded a few loose spikes on one side. The chute, too, was a patchwork of bad repairs. She went around it and thrust the plank up against the other side. There should have been a break, but there was none. The old woman struck the planks a surprised blow and fell back a step. It had all been clear in her mind; just what she had to do. She shot a glance in either direction, accusing the space about her — then dropped the plank. "Hell!" The world had become uncanny for a moment — until she got things back in order and told herself aloud: "I fixed that the other day. What's getting to be the matter with me?" She struck the chute a peevish blow, hung the hammer on it by the claws and turned to the open pasture.

It was a gray, untidy morning, cold and overcast again. In summer, the land crowded up around her, but in winter it fell away. It was still distant. Only calendars brightened towards May; the weather hung in March.

Maybe better look at them cows, thought Etta. Might be a heifer or two having trouble with a calf. **Get that colt in too; work on him.** Get him broke before branding and haying.

Going back to the house, she took the pickup and drove out through the west pasture. There was a swale and then a low hill, after which the ground flattened for a quarter of a mile, to the edge of the brakes. The old Hicks land. Hicks, a homesteader, had come and gone in Etta's lifetime, and now the land was hers. It had associations which nibbled at her mind, but she scarcely paid attention to them now. She passed a hole, caved in and weed-grown for forty-odd years — it had been Hick's cellar. She had almost driven into it once, blinded by the sun. In other years, she had dumped tin cans and dead calves there.

Just beyond where the buildings had stood, the ground had been broken. The truck rocked over a slight ridge. Buffalo grass had returned substantially to the one-time field, but there were patches of tall growth, and sunflowers made strong stands around anthills. There had been fences here and there, too, but it was no longer possible to tell just how they had run.

Etta came to the brakes and turned along them. Some hundred head of stock were scattered over this part of the pasture. Etta calculated the proportion of calves in the herd. It was the heifers, bred a bit later in the summer, who were calving now, with a few of the oldest cows. Some years she had kept the young ones back, breeding them when they were two-year-olds. But lately she had neglected to do that, and invariably some of them had trouble. She was not surprised to discover one such animal before the tour was over. The calf's front feet had emerged.

The cow went into a draw as the old woman approached. She parked the pickup and got a rope from the box. The heifer stopped between two cottonwoods at the bottom of the draw. There Etta succeeded in throwing a loop over her head. The animal didn't know she was caught until Etta took a wrap around the tree and tightened the rope. Fighting took the cow's breath, and soon Etta had her snubbed close.

Eyes rolling white and throat wheezing hard, the creature, orange in her winter coat, sank to the sand. Her young body trembled. The old woman set about her midwife's task. It was no easy work, although the heifer's problem was less serious than some Etta had had to put in the chute back at the place. Alone there, but for the cow, and the calf to be born, the old woman struggled —and felt her heart labor uncertainly, while her lungs gasped always for more air. Yet her concentration was almost fully upon the calf. She paused only to renew her strength; then gave herself unsparingly to her effort once more. Soft curses blew off her lips because she was not younger, and because pain began to nip at her chest.

Soon she rested again, sighing, taking time to look around her at the draw, from whose shale sides she had occasionally picked the fossil shells of sea creatures from a time so remote it boggled her mind. But now the great barrel of the mother animal heaved rhythmically, swelling the vital passage and only opening to the future of her kind, so far removed from the primordial, germinative sea, on whose dead sediments the drama was enacted. Etta's labor and the cow's moved the microcycle to fulfillment: the warm, wet head came forth, not dead, not yet aware of life. The heifer groaned. Her body lurched with one tremendous moment. The steaming calf quivered in Etta's arms — she, fallen back, sat on the cold ground. Etta's hand moved over the ribs, gaunt sides and bony rump. She stayed there, holding the calf, rubbing hard with her gloves. As she rubbed, the hair became rich and crisp. The calf's face was a mass of tight curls. Its ears, which had at first lain rabbit-like along its neck, wagged forward. Now its body pulsed with little starts, but it didn't know what to do. Etta got it to its feet. It took a step and collapsed. Etta, slapping at her cramped legs, managed to stand.

She got the cow up and once more lifted the calf. Walking it between her legs, she guided it to the udder. Its head went up, but it sought blindly for the tit. Its mouth worked with a smacking sound; it braced its feet. The tiny, humped body swayed, quaking uncertainly. The little mouth caught one of Etta's fingers and squeezed hard, with a new surge of effort. She managed to replace the finger with a tit.

Then she stepped, almost staggered, backwards. It'll be all right now, she thought. For quite a while she stood there, letting the calf suck while its mother was still tied, but also trying to breathe away the pain in her chest. Finally she loosened the rope and pulled it off. The heifer sniffed at her calf and let it suck more. Etta was satisfied. Sometimes heifers wouldn't claim their first offspring, but this one's instincts were right.

The calf finished sucking and turned from its mother. Still on uncertain feet, it explored the world two yards away, facing the black hillside and the thin capricious breeze. Budding cottonwoods rattled their sap-filled twigs, and brush like sticks and Spanish bayonets tore the timeless currents, shivering stunned and repetitive.

Etta got the rope and started for the pickup. She had to stop and rest several times. Once she looked back. The cow and calf had lain down close beside each other. And so she faced the hill, her mind considering only the obstacle it presented. Above the shale it was rocky; gravel disclosed big lichen-covered rocks and myriad small ones, some of them quite prettily colored. Sparse grass, occasionally touched with green, struggled amid the Spanish bayonets and coarse barren patches. At the top, the good black soil was cut straight up and down. It was about a foot through, and showed the exposed roots of buffalo grass curling back protectively.

When she got to the pickup, Etta finished her inspection of the herd. Her eyes took in each animal — head, barrel, legs — to measure its health and judge whether it had calved. Often she stopped the pickup, wrapping her arms over the steering wheel and studying the blockish, white-faced Herefords. Some animals threw up their heads with bovine surprise. Others searched restlessly for the new green shoots.

She drove along the brakes, looking for more calving heifers. But, weary already, she didn't leave the pickup. If they're in the bushes, she thought, they'll have to take care of themselves.

At the south fence, she cut round and headed north-eastward. Her bull pasture was north of the place, and the horses were there too. During the spring she kept close watch on the bulls and checked the fences. Keppler's pasture bordered her on the east. Obligingly he put his cows is a south pasture along the state highway during the season, but even so, a bull might decide to walk through the barbed wire and go visiting.

At one point northwest of the ranch buildings, irregular growth cut a swath across the pasture. Etta slowed the pickup and crossed the swath at an angle. The pickup rocked from side to side. For here, like veins or roots, a maze of old cattle trails, cut so deeply that time and the reconquering buffalo grass could not erase them, converged towards the ranch — towards the point where the old pens had stood when Bick Jimson owned a thousand head of cattle and they ranged from the Cheyenne to the White River. And Etta once at ten, just about here, had galloped into a milling herd with her pony to help Red Arnsdorf cut out some Barrett stock, and a cow had run under the pony's neck, stopping it short, pitching Etta down among heavy legs and hot, startled breaths, terrified, crying out, until from nowhere Bick Jimson appeared on his sleek bay and plucked her up by one arm, setting her in the saddle before him amid his smells of leather and sweat and tobacco. He held her and kept talking until the tears were gone and she laughed: "You don't want to bulldog them cows. You just bulldog steers. By golly! I didn't know I had a little bulldogger. I'm going to put you in the rodeo." And then he put her back on her pony.

She took the rocking motion of the pickup in her body, slouched over the wheel, her left hand gripping it low, her right arm wrapped over the top. She saw the trails bare and fresh, saw the milling herd. But these images passed like drifters on horseback through the landscape of her mind, and when the trails were behind her, she looked for the bulls. She opened a wire gate and then approached a swale. There the thick-set registered sires grazed toward her in a ragged line. All eight were there, and so she swung along the fence. It was an old fence, but the three strands of barbed wire, if rusted, were tight and good. The posts were a curious mixture. Every third one was an old cedar post that had rotted off and been reset. The tops of these came only to the top strand of wire. Newer pine posts interspersed the cedars, and there were a few steel posts. All this variety gave the fence a crippled, untidy appearance. Etta didn't like it. She hadn't liked it for years, but there it was.

Half way down the fence she met Keppler. He was on horseback; a dark, sturdy bay with a blazed face. She stopped the pickup and climbed out.

Keppler sat heavily in the saddle, a man of forty, not fat, not tall, but large-framed. "Howdy!" He had a squarish face and two-day's growth of whiskers.

"Howdy!"

They shouted at each other, habituated to speaking through wind out of doors.

"You ordering this weather?" he asked.

"Me ordering it? Hell!" Etta was both peeved and pleased by the kidding. She took hold of the fence. Instead of looking at each other, they both looked downwind.

Keppler said: "If it was mine to do, I'd see that the damned weather man was fired."

Etta's mind was elsewhere. "Goddamned if I didn't have to help a heifer this morning. Same thing every year."

"Hell you say? They can be bad business. Same time, a man can't afford to keep them another year with no calf. Way prices are."

"When you figuring on moving them down?" To the basin, she meant.

"Not till the weather breaks. I ain't even branded yet." He unzipped his duck jacket halfway and dug tobacco and papers from his shirt pocket. In the shelter of the split zipper, he began to work at a cigarette. Wind swirled half the tobacco from his paper.

Etta said: "Everything's late as hell this year." Then, irritation sharpened her voice. "You checking on my bulls, huh?" because she knew that was why he was there, and probably his concern was justified.

"They stay to home damned good." Keppler licked the paper and rolled the cigarette between his fingers.

Keppler's half the fence was new and had four wires. Etta looked down her stumbling rank of posts. "I'm going to put this fence all in new." She tapped her fingers on a stub of cedar. "Like to get all that south fence rebuilt too, before I croak." Then she looked up at Keppler. Eyes narrow, cheeks drawn slightly, he kept his gaze toward the horizon.

The pain in Etta's chest, which had faded or been forgotten, came back with a devilish twinge. She imagined he thought she was crazy. Trying to build anything up now. It made her want to snap at him. Alone, she could deal with it, but in the presence of another, death became intimate, invading her with the private knowledge that there had been much she hadn't understood when she sat by her dad's death bed, too close to see, listening to him say: "I should have stayed there more. I got mixed up about it. The place is what I really cared about. I want it to go on. You look after it. The hon-yockers can't last. You build the ranch back; you're the one that's stayed with it." And she, too anguished to cry, had said: "I will, Dad. I **will**." After the homesteaders had fenced up the open range, leaving just the two sections Bick Jimson owned: one for her and one for Melanie, Carrie's daughter. She hadn't seen herself on his bed then; she was his immortality. And she **had** built it back. Alone.

The horse put out his nose to her hand. The wind gusted urgently against her. The vague pasture was dry and empty. She had images of Red Arnsdorf, who built the original fence — with ric-rac wire and the cedar posts, which he had cut. He had looked like a man near death — and he was. But he had built a fence to divide the land, and now she ought to build it all new. In this moment, it seemed terribly important to make it high and strong — four wires, **five!** and posts that would last forever.

"It'll soon be time to turn out the bulls," Keppler ventured. "But if you want to work on the fence, I'll help you. I'll give you a hand, if you do it when I ain't haying or something. I got a boy; he could dig the holes maybe."

Etta studied him. She saw him when he was a boy. The old man Keppler had grabbed the section his horse stood on in 1939. She still didn't know where he had got the money, but she had had her eye on the land. The old man hadn't amounted to a hill of beans before that — he had come after the homesteaders — and she had looked down on them. Yet had had respect for them too. They were clean, hard-working people. This one's wife kept a nice house; she'd been in it once. They were a family: there was a son and a daughter. The idea of their perpetuity encroached, and her feelings closed against accepting their help.

"I got to hire someone pretty soon," she said. "There's stuff to be done: haying and branding."

"Yeah," he nodded — then added: "You should take it kind of easy."

"Hell!" she exploded, "as if I could! Got no end of work. I'm going to have to run in that colt of mine and break him. I need a young horse. Have to have one to ride in the Badlands this summer. That Gypsy's getting too old." Something was wrong with what she had said, and she scowled up at Keppler, making it his fault. Then she got it straight. "Gypsy! Hell, Gypsy's been dead for years! I'm talking about that Spangle horse." She dropped her eyes. Memory had caught her off guard, and it was a dirty trick. For Gypsy had died the winter she moved out on the couch. She had watched her die with a gut-level sense that the same thing would happen to her one day — and visions of immortality fared poorly in the bleak Dakota winter.

"Time . . . sure flies," offered Keppler.

She looked up to nod at him. The commonplace phrase helped to put things back in order. "Seems last year I broke Spangle. Now I got to break another one."

"Be careful of him."

"Oh, his mother was a good horse. He'll turn out all right." Their eyes met then, and she saw what he had really meant. "Lad, I was breaking horses before you was born!"

He dropped his chin in a nod.

But he had been right, and her crankiness grew. "Guess I better be getting on. A person could chew the fat all day. Never get nothing done."

Still, she did not leave right away. Their talk ran to Potter, who was breeding Angus cattle to Hereford bulls. Keppler himself was introducing Angus into his strain, because the dark pigment kept the tits from getting sore if it snowed and then the sun came out strong.

These were new ideas, and Etta could see that they were good ideas, but she had no feel for them. She had no plan to introduce Angus into her herd.

"The calves are bigger, too," Keppler went on.

That made Etta angry, and something inside her said Keppler wanted to dig her about her calves. "That's a lot of nonsense!" she snapped. Searching for an argument, she went on: "You don't get a bigger calf without feeding him more. So it works out the same in the end."

"Feeding them's what we're here for," he said, but he had pulled back a little.

She only grunted.

He was silent for half a minute. Then he started again, saying: "Myles is vaccinating for vibriosis this year. I wonder if we shouldn't all do that?"

"I ain't never vaccinated for nothing but blackleg," said Etta. "They ought to quarantine cattle bringing that stuff in."

"Ain't that detectable. We cattlemen got to look out for ourselves, ain't we?"

"They quarantined hoof and mouth disease back in the 1880's — put a quarantine line between here and Texas so they couldn't bring them cattle in. They could do it if they wanted to."

Keppler was looking at her strangely, blinking, but she felt she had made a point about her dad's time, before any Keppler ever heard of South Dakota.

Satisfied, she said: "Got to hightail it. Got a **hell** of a lot of work to do."

"Yeah. Yeah! Me too."

In her pickup again, she felt the surge of a deep and hostile pride. Sitting straight, with a fierce jaw, she sped away. The Jimson name had come to this country first, and it couldn't make a difference what others did, or what they knew. Although she accepted her neighbors' ownership and rights in every legal and personal way, on another plane she felt their presence to be transitory. Only the name "Myles" rode uncomfortably with her. Beside him, she was a small owner. That insidious intangible the corporate owner oughtn't to exist.

She drove past the bulls, and they threw up their heads. She had caked them with the pickup, but that was already some time ago, and now they were apparently unsure of their interest and soon went on searching for the green shoots.

Just north of the bulls was another weed-grown hole, almost identical with the one on the Hicks land. Around it Etta had occasionally found remnants of shoes and rusted out pans. There had been nine Welke children. One Welke girl had frozen to death somewhere west of the place — the one folks said had never been right after the old man held her head under water in a washtub to punish her. But this sweep of regrown prairie seemed reluctant to admit ghosts — unless the ghosts of Etta's memory. The surviving Welke "kids" were grandparents now, scattered from Aureole City to California. They had countless grandchildren — thirty or forty. Etta had the land, and looked out of her aging flesh upon its timeless silence with only a passing thought of what it meant that a group of human beings had struggled through birth and death here, accomplishing just the maintenance of life over a span of years. Because her own life had been hard, and in a way she still blamed the homesteaders for that, she wasted no pity on the weed patch that had been a home. Although a child at the time, she had known the free range; she had been born to other dreams.

Farther north yet, the horses grazed near the brakes. The ground sloped and became rocky. There were numerous prairie cactuses. She swore, with a thought that the spines might puncture her tires. But she made no effort to avoid them.

There were just four horses: Spangle and Star and two unnamed geldings — generally referred to as "that big devil," and "that U-necked sonofabitch." They watched her approach. Both geldings were broke to ride but rarely ridden. When she got round them, they strung out at a run, heading for the place. It was almost two miles in now. When they got there, Etta herded them into the corral with the pickup. Then she let all but the colt out again.

She fastened the gate and got a lariat.

"Whoa, there, Star."

He stood across the corral facing her, ears forward, eyes wide.

"Easy now, boy." She held the rope behind her and put out one hand, walking slowly forward.

He was a rich brown color, with a squashed, four-pointed star in the middle of his forehead. His mane and tail, hooves and shanks, were black. He was not big, and not going to get too big — a good saddle horse, lean and yet sturdy. He was lively, and yet gentle when caught. And he was a handsome animal, with a nicely shaped head.

"There, boy," said Etta. But when she got close, he wheeled, throwing up bits of manure, and galloped around her to the opposite fence, skidding to a stop, front feet wide. "Why you dirty rascal!" she called after him. Once more she approached slowly, rope hidden, hand outstretched. "Nice horse. Whoa, boy, whoa there."

He stood with his rump toward her this time, watching back out of one eye, but sniffing a corral pole, as if it were all that interested him.

"There, boy. There boy. Just hold steady now."

Her hand was three inches from his croup when he began to shiver — he sprang suddenly to one side and galloped round to the opposite fence.

"Why you double-crosser!" she yelled, shaking a fist. "I ought to bust a two-by-four over you. Long-legged sonofabitch! You run away from me! Think you're damned cute, don't you?"

She started for him again, speaking softly: "Nice horse. Steady boy. Good Star. Good boy."

This time he pranced around her, head and tail high, before she even got near.

Etta threw the lariat on the ground and stood, hands on hips, facing the animal. "All right. I'm going to break you to ride if I croak doing it. You want to be here till hell freezes over? I'm going to have a saddle on you, you bastard, so you might as well hold still."

Etta's Funeral

The funeral was set for 1:30 on Thursday, and the weather turned out to be quite hot. Tad Ridley went to Haywood's Chapel by himself and parked in the lot at the rear. The small anteroom had a few chairs and a settee on one side. Pete Olsen and his wife occupied the latter, and two white-haired men Tad didn't know were in chairs nearby. He hadn't expected to see strangers here but then guessed that they were cowhands Etta might have known years ago. Now very likely they lived in obscure hotels or boarding houses, emerging only for funerals, as if in rehearsal for their own passing.

Tad signed the register and entered the chapel. A woman played soft, rather pleasant organ music off in the left-hand corner. A lectern stood nearby. The pews were blond in finish, the walls plain, and the whole room illuminated by a clear but quiet light. The casket, in a simple, arched alcove at the front, decorated with a single wreath of flowers, was neither obvious nor obscure; Tad had no feeling except a feeling of strangeness. He sat toward the back, fingering a little hymnal that had been given him at the door, eyeing the closed casket with a sense that it was a kind of altar, cast from iron and solid through.

Other people came in now: the Olsens, the Kepplers and Tad's parents among them. His parents did not see him and went to another pew. When the two old men came in, one of them sat beside Tad. His breath was heavy with alcohol.

The chapel filled substantially, but there were no mourners. This disturbed Tad. He felt himself a mourner, yet barred by usage from the role. He felt conspicuous, although no one knew that he had inherited the ranch. It surprised him that so many people had come.

They increased his sense of wonderment. His position seemed even stranger. What right have I to **her** land? he asked himself. He couldn't get hold of anything.

For three months he had been Etta Jimson's hired man. His highest aspiration had been to run a few cows with her bunch — she had made that offer. And he had been aware that she was paying close attention to everything he did. Her careful observation had made him uneasy. Then, after her heart attack, she had asked him if he would look after things. There was nothing to say but yes. He had thought she meant until she was better. But apparently she had known what was coming — the will was dated just a few days before her death. He was left with an uncanny sense of her: the way she had looked at him, spoken to him. It was as if she had been — in some way he could not plumb or wholly assent to — in love with him. Now the place was his. Owning a ranch had been an exciting dream, a safe reverie. What was the reality? There in the chapel, all feeling seemed to be arrested. He was neither happy over his gain nor especially sad over Etta's death.

More elderly people came in, most of them strangers to Tad. The men seemed to feel awkward and out of place, as they might have been at a grade-school Christmas program. Etta hadn't visited these people or been visited by them while Tad worked for her. Yet they must have been aware of her, and her passing had summoned them forth.

At 1:30, the pall bearers came in and took seats up front. A minister, the Reverend Ellery Williams according to the paper, went to the lectern — a fairly tall man with a self-possessed air. The least suggestion of a smile flirted about his mouth. Tad at first thought this inappropriate, but it made him inwardly comfortable, and he smiled a little, imagining himself conducting the service.

The minister began with a prayer, but it was lost to Tad, for Mrs. Olsen, sitting behind him, was whispering to Pete. "What kind of a preacher is he? He ain't got a collar on."

"Damned if I know," Pete answered. "There's so many of them these days."

Next came a hymn. Tad didn't sing, but Mrs. Olsen did. Vigorously. Tad was able to follow the words with her all right, but her tune seemed to be "Jingle Bells."

When the song was finished, and they sat down again, the minister arranged some note cards and looked over the gathering, speaking with a quiet, personal tone that made the occasion seem a natural part of life. The thought that it could be was a discovery for Tad.

"Loretta Elizabeth Jimson, known to her friends as Etta, was born on the 5th of May, in the city of Mitchell. She lived from infancy near Pinnacle on the ranch built by her father, Bickford Jimson, a pioneer cowman. The family is counted among a handful of original settlers who were in Western South Dakota when the homesteaders came and remained after the fencing and plowing of the land. Her passing is an historical moment, the end of an epoch, and we gather here as we should to mark the season of her death. Let us mourn her as becomes this season, for Ecclesiastes tells us there is a time to mourn. Yet an end is always a beginning; the same text says: 'One generation passeth away, and another generation cometh: but the earth abideth for ever.' A funeral is an occasion for paying respects to the one who will no longer be among us. Yet in the inward way that he individually does so, each of us expresses himself: a funeral is in truth a pause during which the living become conscious of life, this uncanny power, which, like a good saddlehorse, will bear us unerringly home in darkness if we have guided it carefully in the outward journey by daylight. The deepest honor we can pay the deceased is proper mourning for her — not mistaken mourning for her epoch or (saddest of all) mourning for ourselves. To mourn for Etta is to dwell briefly in the reality of her absence, so that an understanding of it may become part of us. But to mourn for the epoch is to refuse the responsibility of our own portion, and to mourn for ourselves is nothing less than to confess the failure of our vision. We are transients in this existence, the terms of which were negotiated through the dim eons of the past. Too easily we may look upon Etta and the hard struggle of her life and conclude that all is vanity and vexation of spirit, and there is no profit under the sun. But the Preacher also said 'there is nothing better, than that a man should rejoice in his own works; for that is his portion.' I believe that Etta rejoiced in her work; I believe that we should return to rejoice in ours. We are neither inwardly free nor outwardly determined; rather we are the vehicles of a divine impulse and at one with it through rejoicing. Thereby we unfold more truth than an academy of scientists, who may tell us everything about our bodies but nothing about our souls. Implicit in a funeral service is the question of Job: 'If a man die, shall he live again?' That is the question in our hearts, and the one we must answer before we can have an intimation of what in fact we are. Everything we do, feel, value and concern ourselves with is governed by our unconscious assumptions about what man is. If the spirit dies with the body, we must accept man's recent image as an absurd creature alienated from his world, driven by impersonal needs. But if life is eternal, its meaning is invested in spiritual growth, the personal value of which implies a universal reverence for mankind and leads to a glimpse of the cosmic meaning of a 'person' — man becomes a significant being by definition. However, immortality cannot be proved (neither, of course, can it be disproved) — and in this scientific age, we are greatly concerned with demonstrability; we are impatient with the 'hocus-pocus' of religion. We place our faith in our science, and indeed there are areas in which it is appropriate that we should do so. But is it acceptable to dismiss that which does not suit the laboratory? Immortality seems occult, magical, and therefore dubious. But does it in fact seem more improbable than the world we now inhabit; more miraculous than our present experience of selfhood? If we look upon ourselves and our world without awe, without a constant sense of wonder at what we see, it is perhaps because science has led us to believe all this can be explained. Unfortunately, however, science has generally turned away from all that which **it cannot explain** — and it has even divorced us from the explicable by familiarizing us through abstraction; we are familiar with our world through names and dimensions and functions, but 'Little we see in Nature that is ours!' This is the paradox of our time: in our obsession with analyzing the material world, we have forgotten the **fact** of it; in mastering **things,** we have forgotten the miracle of their being. 'Where is the wisdom we have lost in knowledge?' asked Eliot. And Wordsworth, the famous Romantic poet, wrote: 'The world is too much with us; late and soon,/ Getting and spending, we lay waste our powers.' Better to be a pagan, he said. Probably the pagan had no difficulty believing in his own immortality; man's sense of an undying soul is almost universal in his primitive experience — a knowledge deeper than reason. There is more to us than we know! In an age of finite answers, we have a hard time believing in that which we cannot weigh and touch and taste, but is that not more the mark of our error than the measure of our reality? Let us light a candle rather than curse the darkness. The scientific discoveries that we take for granted would have seemed magical a few centuries ago — can we not then readily believe in the **possibility** of energies inaccessible to our instruments; beyond what we refer to as the physical world?"

Keppler now had his leg out in the aisle, tapping his toe against the pew ahead of him with a hesitant beat, like a woodpecker that needed rewinding. Everyone was aware of it but him. Then his wife gave him an elbow in the ribs, and he jerked his foot back, tucking it under his seat and crossing the opposite ankle to keep it there.

The minister went on: " What is man? We know he is the product of a billion or more years of evolution — dinosaur eons through which God seems to have been groping in the dark. Can we think that the invention of man was an accident? Implicit in the fact of his existence is the idea that the fundamental impulsion of life must have had him somehow as its objective. And if we consent to that, must we not also accept that this invisible force equally intends — even is one with — his love, that highest efflorescence of his being, to which his body and his reasoning power are in their separate ways as an age of reptiles; the concretions from which the higher phenomenon is able to derive? Such an argument may fare poorly in the laboratory, but there is more to man that the test tube can measure; more to him than his rational self. A mad man may be someone who has lost everything but his reason. Man is able to experience a selfhood beyond the reasoning mind, which reason both serves and builds, but which love tells us is not interdependent with reason and the body. In one of Dostoyevsky's great novels, a 'lady of little faith' asks an elder how she can get back her faith in the life beyond the grave. As a child, she believed only mechanically. 'How,' she asks, 'how is one to prove it?' And the elder responds: 'There is no proving it, though you can be convinced of it . . . by the experience of active love. Strive to love your neighbor actively and indefatigably. In as far as you advance in love you will grow surer of the reality of God and of the immortality of your soul. If you attain to perfect self-forgetfulness in the love of your neighbor, then you will believe without doubt, and no doubt can possibly enter your soul. This has been tried, This is certain.' What is meant by love? It is an approving way of engaging that which is Other; it is a form of knowledge. We find ourselves separated, alienated, from others and from the world — this is a necessary consequence of the individuation which makes higher consciousness possible. Love, then, is that **dwelling-in** others — and the world, for things are important too — which **re-unites** us: we lose ourselves and gain the sense of at-oneness with eternal principles. Etta Jimson lived alone, but she **dwelled-in** the ranch, the land, and this was a form or re-union, a way of knowing, a door to the spirit's growth. These old-timers pitted themselves against the raw country. I do not say that everything they did was good, yet, within the sweep of history, they became the reality of our past. They made a world for us. It is for us to look ahead; it is for us to ask what we will make of that world and of ourselves."

Mrs. Olsen was whispering to Pete again: "I wonder if they're going to open the casket? I want to see if she looks natural."

"Damned if I know," Pete whispered back. "I want to slip out myself."

"I want to see her!" hissed Mrs. Olsen.

"And so," the minister continued, "faced with the question of Job, we must seek the answer in the challenge of ourselves, the challenge of our spiritual growth. During the process of growth, we may fall —through doubt or failure — as we fall when we first learn to walk and return to crawling. But The Fall always discloses new complexity to be mastered. In evolution, there is a necessary coexistence of the higher phenomenon and the lower from which it derives, and this is reflected within the individual. It may explain the seeming contradictory nature of man — his urge to go backward; his urge to go ahead: the beast striving to be a god, and the god that reverts to a beast. But there are those who have explored the new territories in the journey towards love and an affirmative answer to the question of Job — this has been tried; this is certain — look to the saints, prophets of men and letters. But look also to the humble souls, the Etta Jimsons of this world. All her life, she dwelled in the land, held it as her own. Yet, on her death bed, in one final encompassing act of love, she handed it on to the present generation."

Tad straightened. The minister must have talked with Etta's executors — but of course he would have!

Behind Tad, Mrs. Olsen hissed: "Who? Who did she hand it to?"

"In that act," said the minister, "she triumphed. She **knew**. For the conviction that the soul endures comes not from reason or science, but from the full, positive actualization of ourselves — that conviction dwells on the frontier within us. What a piece of work man **is**! And 'the only universe capable of containing the human person is an irreversibly "personalizing" universe.' How can we recognize ourselves as of the very essence of this universe and yet fear it as alien in its mysteries? 'The earth is the Lord's, and the fullness thereof; the world, and they that dwell therein. For he hath founded it upon the seas, and established it upon the floods . . . **This** is the generation of them that seek him.' Let us pray: Eternal God, may we have the wisdom to accept that 'to every thing there is a season, and a time to every purpose under the heaven; A time to be born, and a time to die; a time to plant, and a time to pluck up . . . A time to mourn, and a time to dance.' Receive the soul of Etta Jimson, for now the silver cord is loosed and the golden bowl is broken, and it is written 'then shall the dust return to the earth as it was: and the spirit shall return unto God who gave it.' Amen."

"M-m-m-m! Wasn't that good!" whispered Mrs. Olsen.

"I didn't understand it," muttered Pete. "I liked that Baptist preacher they had last funeral. He made me feel so good I wished I was dead."

They then stood and sang a hymn version of the twenty-third psalm, and then they sat for another prayer. The minister announced that the committal would be held in the vehicle bay at the rear of the mortuary, since the cemetery was not nearby.

A man in a black suit went forward, removed the wreath from the casket and opened it for viewing.

"I don't want to look," whispered Pete. "I'm going to scoot around the other way."

"I'm going to have a peek!" said his wife.

Tad, moving in the line, found himself not wanting to look; not really willing to believe what he would see. He had only been to one funeral before in his life. Lifting his eyes then, he was surprised to find that the event was not startling. A waxen figure with too much color in the face; a shape without the truth of the person.

Behind him, he heard Mrs. Olsen whisper to someone: "Now, don't she look natural!"

The other party, also a woman, answered: "She certainly does! I ain't seen her in twenty years, and she certainly does!"

In the hearse bay at the rear, most of the people gathered in a group. Tad saw a few slip through an exit. His mother smiled at him from a few steps away. She, ignorant of the will, nonetheless seemed full of the occasion, as if it were somehow a Ridley doings. Perhaps his somberness inspired a motherly need to communicate well-being; perhaps, in the presence of death, her own life became a kind of triumph.

Mrs. Olsen was still whispering: "Well, it was a nice service. He said nice things, but I know for a fact that old Bick Jimson used a long rope to do his ranch building. He was a slicker. Who got the place now? Was it et up in debts?"

The casket had been wheeled out at the far end of the bay. Immediately the minister began reading: "I will lift up mine eyes unto the hills, from whence cometh my help. My help **cometh** from the Lord, which made heaven and earth . . ." After the psalm, he said a prayer, and then, very quickly it seemed to Tad, the pallbearers slid the casket out of sight in the hearse. An old man near Tad had a stunned look in his eyes. But Tad still was unable to get hold of his feelings.

Then a young man in black snapped the hearse doors shut with mechanical efficiency, and sudden nausea filled Tad's belly. He made a slight turn; an inchoate gesture of looking for someone. Only Mrs. Olsen was there, talking to his mother now.

"Well, Etta didn't forget us!" said Mrs. Olsen. "She's going to be buried down home."

"I don't understand why," said Tad's mother. "I'd want to be buried in the Aureole cemetery. That's so far away down there."

Tad's father grunted a little laugh. "It ain't far away if you're down there. I think the old gal's right. Close to her ranch. Damned poor soil up here too."

Mrs. Olsen cackled and went out the back way.

Tad said: "I'm in the lot. See you down home later." He wanted to be alone.

The sun was hot, but it felt good. He opened himself to the sickness in his belly, listened to the crush of misery in his head. He was scarcely aware of his trip to the ranch.

When he arrived his eyes searched from the house to the corral. Where was the small, shuffling figure of Etta Jimson? Behind the barn? Out by the stacks? She had been painting on the house and had not quite finished. **Shall I finish it?** Tad asked in his mind. **What shall I do now?** Everything loomed before him: the haying, the branding, the decisions about cross-breeding and feeding yearlings. All was silent. And the swallows were busy with their mud nests at the eaves.

All right, he thought. **All right then. I'll go ahead and work at it. I own it — legally. Maybe in time it'll be mine.**